PENGUIN

THE

Li Ang is the pen name o̶̶̶̶̶̶̶̶ ̶̶̶̶̶̶̶̶ ̶̶was born in Taiwan in 1952. In 1975 she w̶̶̶̶ ̶̶̶̶̶̶̶ ̶̶ed States, where she studied at the University of Or̶̶̶ ̶̶he started writing when she was seventeen and has since published several novels and collections of stories in Taiwan. Today she teaches in the Department of Theatre at the University of Chinese Culture in Taipei. Her home town of Lugang, in central Taiwan, is the setting for *The Butcher's Wife*, her first novel to be translated into English. It won the *United Daily News* fiction contest in 1983.

THE BUTCHER'S WIFE

LI ANG

TRANSLATED FROM THE CHINESE
BY HOWARD GOLDBLATT
AND ELLEN YEUNG

PENGUIN BOOKS

PENGUIN BOOKS

Published by the Penguin Group
Penguin Books Ltd, 27 Wrights Lane, London W8 5TZ, England
Penguin Books USA Inc., 375 Hudson Street, New York, New York 10014, USA
Penguin Books Australia Ltd, Ringwood, Victoria, Australia
Penguin Books Canada Ltd, 10 Alcorn Avenue, Toronto, Ontario, Canada M4V 3B2
Penguin Books (NZ), Ltd, 182–190 Wairau Road, Auckland 10, New Zealand

Penguin Books Ltd, Registered Offices: Harmondsworth, Middlesex, England

First published in Taiwan, under the title *Sha Fu*, 1983
This translation first published in the USA by North Point Press 1986
First published in Great Britain by Peter Owen 1989
Published in Penguin Books 1991
1 3 5 7 9 10 8 6 4 2

Printed in England by Clays Ltd, St Ives plc

TRANSLATORS' NOTE

The publication in Taiwan of *The Butcher's Wife* was a significant literary event of 1983; awarding first prize in the annual *United Daily News* island-wide contest for long fiction to this novella was a courageous statement for literary freedom that earned the newspaper and the contest judges far more opprobrium than praise. Indignant critics, government officials, and self-styled defenders of the public morality were outraged that such an honor could be bestowed on a work that they considered little more than pornographic. The controversy over *The Butcher's Wife* has since died down (although the author, Li Ang, has recently written an even more "objectionable" work), but the Taiwan literary scene, and contemporary Chinese literature in general, has been lastingly affected by the appearance of this daring and powerful work.

Deciding that *The Butcher's Wife* should be made available to an English-speaking audience was easy; deciding how to accomplish this goal required more thought. Ultimately, a collaborative translation—two genders, two ethnic backgrounds, and two native languages—seemed particularly appropriate for this short novel, which is unique in the Chinese literary tradition, and is the vehicle for such powerful emotions. In our translation, the third on which we have collaborated, we have striven to convey not only the narrative text of *The Butcher's Wife* (for which a literal title would be "Kills Husband," itself a cultural non sequitur), but also the texture—the sharp edges, the sense of brutality that runs throughout the work, and the controlled anger. We have been aided in our work by several colleagues and friends who have read and commented upon it, including Robin Gadjusek, Beata Grant, and, especially, Ruthanne Lum McCunn. To them and all the others, our heartfelt thanks.

AUTHOR'S PREFACE

After receiving my M.A. degree from an American university in 1977, I decided to see some of the country before returning to Taiwan, so I traveled around the United States for the better part of a year. It was during that time, at the California home of a friend, that I happened upon a book in which a news item about the sensational murder of a man by his wife in Shanghai in the 1930s had been reprinted.

What drew me to this particular story of husband killing was the fact that it was not just another case of adultery. In traditional Chinese society, any woman who kills her husband is presumed to have done so because of an extramarital affair; there could be no reason for committing the heinous crime of killing her own husband other than the desire to be with her lover. This demeaning attitude toward the moral character of women has been held by Chinese for thousands of years: any woman guilty of killing her husband is a promiscuous woman, and no other interpretation is possible.

But in this particular sensational case from Shanghai in the 1930s, the accused murderess insisted that she had killed her husband only to escape his abuses and that she was innocent of any extramarital involvements; the prosecution was unable to prove the existence of a "lover." Thus, instead of being just another in a long line of women labeled promiscuous by society, the husband-killer in this case was a woman who had suffered the oppression of traditional society.

I wanted to use this item as the basis of a story, but since I knew virtually nothing about Shanghai, I abandoned my plans. It wasn't until several years later, after I had returned to Taiwan, that I decided to move the setting of the story to my hometown of Lugang, a small seacoast town in central Taiwan that had once been the island's second largest city but was now just another small town that retained the flavor of "old Taiwan." And so, the basic elements of a sensational murder case that had actually occurred in Shanghai were transported to Taiwan and transformed into a story of old Taiwanese society.

I cannot deny that I approached the writing of *The Butcher's Wife* with a number of feminist ideals, wanting to show the tragic fate that awaited the economically dependent Taiwanese women living under the rules of traditional Chinese society. But as I wrote, I found myself becoming more and more concerned with larger issues of humanity, such as hunger, death, sex. What I want to emphasize here is that the ultimate concern of a piece of "feminist literature" is, after all, human nature.

In writing *The Butcher's Wife* I owe the greatest debt of gratitude to my hometown of Lugang; were it not for the many special charms of that place, this story would never have been written.

Naturally, I want also to thank the translators, who have made this work available to a new group of readers.

THE BUTCHER'S WIFE

NEWS REPORT #1

Date:_____, 19___

On the morning of _____, Chen Lin Shi, a woman in her twenties, murdered her husband, Chen Jiangshui, a pig butcher in his forties, in the couple's home in the Chencuo district of northern Lucheng. Using the victim's own butcher knife, she dismembered his body, chopping it up into eight pieces, which she placed in a rattan basket for later disposal. Fortunately, a watchful neighbor discovered the crime and reported it to the police before she could carry out her plan.

When asked why she had killed her husband, Chen responded that he had been a cruel, brutal man who went out to drink and gamble every day, then came home and amused himself by yelling at and beating her. Knowing how she hated to see living things killed, he once forced her to go with him to the slaughterhouse to watch him work. On the day of the crime, he had returned home with a butcher knife and a scowl so menacing that she had feared for her own safety. Toward dawn, after making sure he was fast asleep, she cut him up like a pig, just as she had seen him do at the slaughterhouse. In her own mind this deed also served to avenge the deaths of the countless poor animals that had met their end at his hand.

Chen Lin Shi's confession defies reason and logic, for, since ancient times, a murder of this sort has always been the result of an adulterous affair. We urge the authorities to launch a thorough investigation to determine the identity and precise role of the secret lover in this case. There are those who believe that Chen became mentally unbalanced, that after watching her husband butcher pigs for so long she developed a persecution complex that forced her into butchering him. But the killing of a man by his wife is a moral issue that affects all of society; such an offense cannot be condoned by reason of insanity. The authorities must treat this case with the utmost severity in order to stem the public outcry and restore healthy social tendencies.

NEWS REPORT #2

Although an investigation failed to turn up any secret lover in the sensational murder case of Chen Lin Shi, she was nonetheless sentenced to death for the heinous crime of killing her own husband. In accordance with popular demand and time-honored tradition, Chen was bound and placed on the back of a truck. Eight prison guards and a man sounding a gong then escorted her through the streets of the city to the prison at Tainan. Among the throngs lining the route there were complaints that the parade would have been more exciting if Chen had been an attractive woman, or if a secret lover had been found.

Even without proof of her infidelity, the public exhibition of an adulteress-murderess can serve as a warning against immorality, and in the final analysis, the parading of Chen Lin Shi was a necessity. Surely all the women who saw her will take heed and refrain from imitating foreign women, who are always clamoring for equality and the right to attend Western schools. Such demands are actually little more than excuses for a woman to leave house and home and make a public spectacle of herself. They comprise a mockery of the code of womanly conduct and destroy our age-old concepts of womanhood.

We hope that the parade will inspire concerned citizens to redouble their efforts in the fight to stop the decline in womanly virtues.

CHAPTER ONE

The murder of Chen Jiangshui by his wife, Chen Lin Shi, caused quite a sensation in the town of Lucheng. Despite insistent speculation by the press and the detectives in charge of the case that there must have been a secret lover, local opinion had it that the entire sordid affair was actually a case of Lin Shi's mother reaching for revenge from beyond the grave.

Lin Shi's grandfather had been a man of modest means in Lucheng, a "scholar" who had taught in a family school. Unfortunately, a generation later, Lin Shi's father, who had tuberculosis and no appreciation for farming, sold off all his land to pay for medicine and doctor bills. He died, leaving behind nine-year-old Lin Shi and her mother, a woman not yet thirty.

A widow and a fatherless child—worse yet, not even a male who could at least be expected to carry on the line. Sooner or later the widow would remarry, reasoned one of Lin Shi's uncles, who promptly dispossessed Lin Shi and her mother of the tile-roofed house that was their sole remaining possession, and moved in himself.

In the daytime, mother and daughter were reduced to roaming the streets, foraging for scraps and doing odd jobs just to get by, then sneaking back to the Lin Clan Ancestral Hall at night for shelter. Although now nothing more than a rundown building, this ancestral hall had been erected during the clan's heyday and had been its pride and joy. But time had taken its toll, and whatever could be carted off had already found its way into other clan houses, until virtually all that remained were some pillars, each no bigger around than a single embrace, and a few tiles on the roof.

Since Lin Shi's mother had never exhibited any behavior that would bring shame to the clan, the elders had overridden the objections of some other members and, in the name of charity to widows and orphans, given permission for mother and daughter to take shelter in the ancestral hall.

Then one winter, trouble came. It was a time of war. Who was fighting whom made no difference to the common folk, but the poor harvest that followed in the wake of the unrest did. The stragglers and stray soldiers who frequently drifted into town made life even harder. Lin Shi and her mother, who could no longer find any odd jobs, were close to starvation.

One wintry night just before New Year's Eve, when the bone-chilling weather was the coldest in years and a dazzling full moon hung in the sky, Lin Shi climbed a nearby hill to gather some fallen branches for firewood. Dusk comes and goes so quickly in the winter that in no time at all night had fallen, bleak and desolate. A stiff sea breeze swept across the seacoast town, filling the streets and lanes with blustery howls.

Lin Shi was heading back in the bright moonlight when, from a distance, she saw a tall uniformed man stealthily enter the ancestral hall. A gust of icy wind whipped up the loose ends of his gray leggings and snapped back the brim of his ragged army cap, revealing a young, scarred face.

Lin Shi, who was thirteen at the time, smelled danger. She stood still for a moment to think, then ran for help, her heart gripped by a terrible fear. She ran through the bitterly cold night, stumbling and staggering until she arrived at her uncle's house, where she poured out a rambling, incoherent story.

A soldier! This was no time for heroics, so Uncle rounded up five or six fellow clansmen and neighbors before rushing over to the ancestral hall. Not a word passed among them—they didn't want to scare the soldier off. Creeping up to the door of the side room, they peered through the broken lattices. In the bright moonlight, Lin Shi saw the soldier. He was naked from the waist down, except for a piece of gray legging that was draped loosely around his ankle. Pinned beneath him was her mother, whose face, whose haggard face, was flushed bright red and all aglow with a greedy light.

She was chewing on one rice ball and clutching another in her hand. Low moaning sounds escaped from her mouth, which was stuffed with food. Half-eaten grains of white rice, mixed with saliva, dribbled down the side of her face, onto her neck, and down her shirtfront.

For a fleeting moment, as he was yanked off her, the soldier seemed not to realize what was going on. Once Lin Shi's uncle had assured himself that the man was unarmed, he drove his knee into the soldier's groin. The man clutched himself in pain and crumpled to the ground. All this time, Lin Shi's mother lay in the same position, her underpants pulled down to her knees, her shirt hoisted all the way up, her mouth still chewing greedily. It wasn't until Lin Shi ran up to her that she began to wail, gripping her daughter's hands and fitfully repeating that she had been so hungry, that she had eaten nothing but sweet-potato mash and pig slop for several days, and never enough even of that.

The clansmen and neighbors tied the two adulterers to separate pillars in the ancestral hall. As more and more clansmen began to arrive, they huddled together to decide what to do next. By then, Lin Shi's mother had stopped crying and was whining over and over how hungry she had been, how for the last few days she had eaten nothing but sweet-potato mash and pig slop, how the soldier had offered her two rice balls. She'd been too hungry, that was all, too hungry to think about the consequences.

Through it all, the soldier just stared dejectedly ahead, his blank expression not betraying a single thought. He still hadn't uttered a word. He was quite young, and the scar that ran from his eyebrow to his chin was all that kept him from being handsome.

The heated discussion that erupted failed to produce any decision. One of the clan elders suggested that the adulterous pair be tied to a boulder and thrown into the river—but, of course, that was just an old custom. Someone quickly cautioned the others that since they didn't know which regiment the soldier was attached to, there might be hell to pay later on.

Finally, one of the elders who enjoyed playing the role of mediator took the prudent course of speaking up for Lin Shi's mother, saying that since she had been forced to do what she did, she should not be judged as a common adulteress. Just then, to everyone's surprise, Lin Shi's uncle pushed his way through the crowd, stood right in front of the soldier, and slapped him soundly twice. Then, thumping his own chest, he proclaimed that the Lins were, after all, an honorable family, and if Lin Shi's mother had had any honor at all, she would have resisted to the end and died a chaste woman. Who knows, they might even have erected a memorial arch in her honor. Inexplicably, when the others heard the words "memorial arch," they burst out laughing. By then it was becoming obvious that nothing more was going to happen, so, given the lateness of the hour, the neighbors started drifting off.

The clan elders could see that some sort of decision was needed, and quickly. They glanced meaningfully at Lin Shi's uncle, who knew that Lin Shi had now become the clan's responsibility. After all, he reasoned, they could not allow the Lin family bloodline to be contaminated.

Just before Lin Shi was led away, her mother, who had been whining the same thing over and over, suddenly began to wail and strain at the bonds that held her to the pillar. Lin Shi noticed that even though her mother's clothes were a mess, they didn't seem to be ripped or torn. In fact, the red dress that she was wearing was quite new and in good condition, still showing creases where it had been folded. Then it came to her: That was her mother's wedding dress, which had always been kept at the bottom of the trunk. It was all she had left to wear.

That was to be Lin Shi's last memory of her mother: dressed in red and tied to an ancestral-hall pillar as big around as a single embrace. She never set eyes on her mother again. Now and then a rumor would reach her ears: her mother had drowned in the river during the night. Or her mother and the soldier, after being soundly beaten, had been chased out of Lucheng and told never to return. Or her mother had chosen to run away with the soldier.

The clan elders arranged for Lin Shi to move into her uncle's house, the very same tile-roofed house that had once belonged to her father. But returning to her original home didn't change her life at all. Although the constant warfare never directly involved Lucheng, the unrest and turmoil were never-ending. The harvests were invariably bad, and since Lin Shi's aunt was sick in bed all the time, Lin Shi was responsible for every imaginable chore, inside the house and out. Even then, she was rarely given enough to eat.

Still, over the years, Lin Shi grew into a tall, lanky young woman. She had her mother's long face and long limbs, but all those years of being malnourished had given her an underdeveloped figure that made her look like a doll carved out of a piece of wood. The talk among the neighborhood women was that she was so skinny and flat-chested because her menstrual period had started too late.

Usually, knowledge about this sort of biological change is passed on in private from mothers and elder sisters to the younger girls. But the onset of Lin Shi's menstrual period nearly became a neighborhood joke because she created such a scene when it happened. Not that the women didn't sympathize with her for being motherless and frightened, but they had to laugh when they saw her sprawled out on the floor, screaming, "Save me, I'm bleeding to death!"

Soon after the excitement over her period subsided, Lin Shi took to telling everyone about her most recent dream. It was always: You've seen pillars before, haven't you? Not just any old pillar. No, I mean the kind that's as big around as a single embrace. You know, like the ones in our ancestral hall.

The dream would continue: Several pillars, so tall they impale the clouds, disappearing into a pitch darkness that stretches on endlessly. Suddenly, a rumble of thunder, moving inexorably nearer and nearer. Then a loud boom. Not a trace of flames anywhere, yet the pillars become instantly charred, without so much as wobbling. Finally, after the longest time, dark red blood begins to seep from the cracks in the blackened pillars.

The dream wasn't particularly remarkable to begin with, and

after Lin Shi had repeated it over and over, the neighbors grew so tired of it that as soon as she opened her mouth, they cut her off with, "Here we go with that dream again. I'm sick of hearing it!" Soon, for lack of an audience, Lin Shi stopped talking about her dream altogether. She grew taciturn, often raising her long face in the middle of her work, deep in thought about something only she could fathom.

People eventually interpreted Lin Shi's silence as lovesickness. Only a lovesick person would have that kind of moony expression, the neighbors concluded as they watched her stare foolishly and fixedly at men. In fact, one young fellow said he felt like he was being swallowed up by that hungry gaze of hers.

Lin Shi's uncle had always had plans for her, and if it hadn't been for the other clansmen, he would have sold her on a number of occasions. Now, proclaiming loudly that, like her mother before her, she was in a tearing hurry to get laid, he began to look around anxiously for someone to marry her off to.

He finally settled on a butcher from nearby Chencuo. Though approaching forty, Chen Jiangshui had remained single, for no family in Chencuo was willing to let him marry its daughter. After years and years of slaughtering countless animals, he was visited every night by ghostly pigs bleating on his doorstep. Or so people said. There was also talk among the "Backstreet" ladies that whenever Chen paid a visit, he would make the woman he selected scream like a pig being slaughtered. And so Chen Jiangshui had earned himself a nickname: Pig-Butcher Chen. After a while, hardly anyone remembered his real name.

Given Chen Jiangshui's unsavory reputation and the great difference in age, people began to speculate over the terms of the match, assuming that Lin Shi's uncle must have made himself a pretty good deal. The most popular version was that every ten days or two weeks, Pig-Butcher Chen was to send over a pound of pork. During times of need, food, especially when it was delivered right to the door, was the best betrothal gift of all. No wonder the neighbors all remarked enviously that Lin Shi was able to exchange a body with no more than a few ounces of meat for pork by the pound. Some people had all the luck!

But there was no consensus—no, indeed. Others countered with the argument that Pig-Butcher Chen was merely the person who did the dirty work, not the vendor who peddled the meat, and he was in no position to get, let alone hand out, any pork.

Anyway, Lin Shi had found a husband.

Carrying a small bundle with a few changes of clothing, she crossed Black-Cat Bridge, which spanned the three- or four-meter-wide Black-Cat Gully, and she was in Chencuo. Chen Jiangshui's house was a little farther on, at the edge of Chencuo, within sight of the distant ocean.

Sometime after noon, Lin Shi crossed the threshold and, for the rest of the day, acted the part of a new bride, sitting quietly with her head lowered. Fortunately, Chencuo was on the outskirts of Lucheng, and the people weren't all that mindful of etiquette. In fact, the woman drafted at the last minute to be a token matchmaker had to double as cook. This gave Lin Shi ample opportunity to study her husband: A short, stocky body and a prominent paunch—more fat than a man ought to have—he walked with a sort of waddle, kept his hair cut very short, and had such a sharply sloping crown that the back of his skull seemed to be missing altogether. Fairly ordinary features, except that his small beady eyes were sunk deep into a swelling of flesh around the sockets. Lin Shi was told sometime later that these were known as pig-eyes and that they always belonged to people whose fate was tied to pigs.

That night there was the customary party, which was attended by Lin Shi's uncle, his family, and a few close neighbors and friends of Chen Jiangshui—no more than two or three tables of well-wishers. The guests departed soon after dinner. Lin Shi had hardly eaten a bite all day, so at first she was secretly relieved that the guests had left early. But she hadn't counted on a few of Chen's butcher friends staying behind and downing cup after cup of wine, carrying on until well past midnight. She could hear the sounds of their eating and drinking so clearly through the door curtain that her stomach began to rumble. She forced herself to bear the hunger as she waited for the last few guests to leave, but exhausted and famished, she was close to collapse.

Drunk though the groom was when he came to bed, he insisted on fulfilling his conjugal obligation, causing Lin Shi to exhaust with pitiful screams what little energy she had left. Her screams of pain were so loud and lasted so long, according to her neighbors, that some people who heard them above the whistling night winds took them to be the bleating of ghostly pigs.

When it was over, Lin Shi was nearly in a dead faint. Chen Jiangshui, who was an old hand at this, quickly forced some wine down her throat, and she came around at once, choking hard. Still groggy, she complained that she was hungry. Chen Jiangshui went into the living room and came back with a big piece of pork, dripping with fat, which he stuffed into her mouth, skin and all. With bloated cheeks, she chewed on the pork, making squishing noises as fat oozed out the corners of her mouth and dribbled down in rivulets to her chin and neck, all greasy and wet. Just then her tears finally brimmed over and ran down her face, sending a chill through her.

How could she have guessed that in the days to come this was what her life was going to be like, day in and day out?

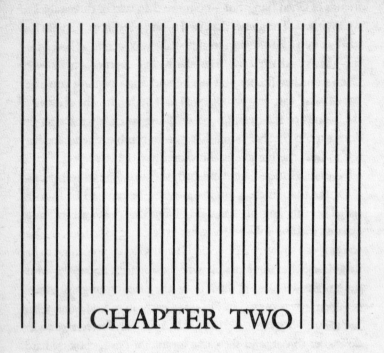

CHAPTER TWO

When it came to being a butcher, Chen Jiangshui was the best around. He came to the slaughterhouse to do odd jobs when he was barely ten years old, or so the story went, and he was soon given his chance to use a knife. The very first time he wielded the twelve-inch, narrow, pointed butcher knife, he plunged it into the pig's gullet swiftly, mercilessly, accurately, his hand never so much as wavering. The butchers in the slaughterhouse took to calling him Pig-Butcher Chen, partly in jest over the way he handled women, but also in concession to his skills.

All those years as a butcher had made Chen Jiangshui an early riser. His wedding night was no exception. At a little after three, when the sky was still pitch black, Chen was up and awake. He looked at Lin Shi, who was sound asleep on the other side of the bed. Without rousing her, he got dressed, picked up his butcher knife, and went off to the small marketplace in the center of Chencuo for breakfast. The elderly porridge vendor who catered to the early crowd had already set up two rickety bamboo chairs and heated his great kettle. He greeted Chen Jiangshui familiarly, not missing a chance to tease him: "Even with a brand new bride at home, I still get your business, eh? Can't bear to make her get up, can you? Such a considerate husband!"

Chen Jiangshui just sort of chuckled and muttered under his breath. Taking the porridge, he squatted down on the ground and noisily wolfed down two bowlfuls. Then he stood up and began to make his way through Chencuo toward the slaughterhouse.

The local slaughterhouse, located just south of Lucheng, was surrounded by a big rice paddy. All Chen had to do was follow the path that snaked its way over from Lucheng's famous red-light district, Backstreet, then cross over the rice paddy, walk past the huge pond, and there it was. After electricity came to Lucheng, the townspeople constructed a generator in the area, but still hardly anyone ever went near the place. To make things worse, the path that led up to the slaughterhouse was nearly overgrown with bamboo that had been planted on both sides, making the place even darker and more forbidding. When the wind was up, the rustling sound of the leaves and the irregular shadows the bamboo cast in the moonlight combined to create such gloom that the path, along with the neighboring pond and the slaughterhouse, had long been portrayed in local legends as haunted.

But talk of ghosts had no effect on Chen Jiangshui. Poverty had forced him into this profession as a youngster, and he and a lot of other people who slaughtered pigs for a living were resigned to the fact that they would be consigned to hell for taking all those lives. What then was there to be frightened of in earthbound ghosts and evil spirits, assuming that such creatures existed in the first place? If worse came to worst, the men would just go off with the spirits when they were summoned.

And yet, these men were not total disbelievers, for they had set up an altar of sorts. At the entrance to the slaughterhouse rested a boulder about three meters in height on which the words "Monument to the Souls of Animals" were carved and highlighted with red paint. Joss sticks glowed in an incense burner in front of the boulder twenty-four hours a day. In addition to the required monthly ceremonies, sacrificial rites were conducted on a grand scale each year on the fifteenth day of the seventh month, the day of prayer and worship for the deliverance of all souls.

The slaughterhouse, a brick building in the shape of an **L**, was just beyond the Monument to the Souls of Animals. The long narrow room running down the middle was the killing floor, while a smaller room on the right was used for branding and other purposes. This was also where most of the butchers kept their things.

As soon as he arrived at the slaughterhouse, Chen Jiangshui went directly to the small room to change into a pair of high rubber boots. He seldom wore an apron because, with all his years of experience, his clothes were rarely dirtied by pig's blood. But the layer of water that always accumulated on the floor was another matter, making high boots an absolute necessity.

After putting his things away, Chen Jiangshui entered the killing floor through a connecting door. He was met by a familiar pungent stench that started his adrenaline flowing. With his head held high, he strode onto the killing floor.

Women were already gathered around the well to the right of the entrance, hauling up water. A number of pigs with their legs tightly bound lay on the ground. Since it was still early, the handful of men just stood around passing the time of day. Apart from the few slaughterhouse helpers, these men were owners of meat stalls. It was they who had brought the pigs over, and even though they wouldn't be doing the killing themselves, they were sticking around to supervise things.

One by one the people greeted Chen Jiangshui as he walked over. A couple of the helpers made catcalls, and one old man who lived near Chencuo even aimed a punch at Chen's groin, calling out in a raucous, laughing voice: "So, tell us. What's your woman like?"

"Small and tight, of course. A real good screw," one of the meat vendors said, assuming the solemn tones of a judge delivering his verdict. "Not like that old hag Golden Flower over at Springtime House. You can stick it in her and never touch a thing. It's a bottomless pit!"

The men roared with laughter.

"Once you get your own woman, you don't have to be an old bum no more," a middle-aged helper said with obvious envy. "You got somebody to cook for you and somebody to sleep with you. That's what I call having it made!"

"Having it made?" someone else quickly countered, hooting loudly. "Look at this one over here—so worn out he can't even make it to work on time!"

More laughter followed, but all the taunts managed to get out of Chen Jiangshui were some good-natured curses—"Fuck this, fuck that!"—and he was grinning so broadly that his beady, deep-set eyes narrowed into mere slits.

The racket continued for a while longer, until the lateness of the hour became apparent to everyone. The helpers reluctantly moved off to the side. Two or three of them lifted a pig off the floor and, with a loud "Heave ho," deposited it on one of the brick platforms. These platforms were three or four feet off the ground, their surfaces sloping gradually toward the center, in the shape of a V. Once the hog-tied animal lay on its back in the depression, it was virtually impossible for it to right itself, let alone get away.

Instinctively knowing what was about to happen, the pig began to squeal loudly, and soon all the pigs in the room were squealing pitifully. One of the helpers raised his voice over the din as he asked Chen Jiangshui: "Is this how your woman squealed last night?"

This time, instead of a "Fuck you!" Chen Jiangshui raised his pointed knife in a menacing gesture to the men who were laughing so hard they could barely stand; a couple of them were doubled up, calling for their mothers.

While the men's attention was diverted, the squealing, struggling pig on the platform nearly managed to roll off, but the helpers quickly pressed it back down. Fortunately for them, the V-shape of the platform made their work a lot easier than if the surface had been flat, and order was soon restored following this brief commotion.

It was now time for Chen Jiangshui to move into action. Grasping the animal's snout with his left hand, he jerked its head back to expose the throat, and before anyone even saw his right hand move, the twelve-inch butcher knife was buried in the pig's gullet. Then, with the animal's pitiful squeals as a background, the knife sliced downwards about two inches and reemerged. Blood spurted out.

This was Chen Jiangshui's moment, the surge during which he

discharged the energy that had been accumulating all morning. After the blade had disappeared into the flesh and was about to be withdrawn, in that brief moment before the blood gushed forth, a wave of warm, musky odor would rush toward his knife hand. As soon as this breathlike odor drifted up, Chen Jiangshui knew, without even seeing a drop of blood, that once again the job had been done to perfection.

But that morning, the first after his wedding night, a bilious stomach and the effects of too little sleep left Chen Jiangshui feeling slightly enervated, just enough to cause a momentary hesitation as he raised his knife. No one knew better than he that when he brought his knife down, more than just the death of a pig was involved—the point of entry and the depth of the cut also determined the price of the pork. The meat of a pig whose blood had not been completely drained would be tinged pink, the color of carrion, and might be thought to have come from a pig that had been butchered after it was dead. This was the worst thing that could happen in the pork business.

Luckily for him, it was neither the first nor the fifteenth of the month, nor was it the birthday of some local deity, so there weren't all that many pigs waiting to go under his knife. Using every bit of energy he could muster, and calling upon his many years of experience, Chen Jiangshui got through the day with no real mistakes, even though his knife hand was wet and slippery with sweat, making him feel as though he were holding a handful of warm pig's blood.

Emerging from the slaughterhouse, he heaved a sigh. It was early, just past seven o'clock, and the sun was still shining brightly. As had been his custom for many years, Chen Jiangshui left the slaughterhouse and headed off in the direction of Backstreet. Not until he reached the pond did he remember that he had a new bride at home. For a brief moment he contemplated dropping by Springtime House, as usual, to crawl into Golden Flower's warm, snug bed. But when he recalled how Lin Shi had screamed the night before, he made a detour and walked toward Chencuo with heightened anticipation.

Lin Shi had obviously just got up, for she was leaning against the bed combing her hair, her back toward the door. Chen Jiangshui was surprised to discover that this skinny woman of his had such a luxuriant head of silky black hair. He quickened his steps and approached her from behind. Grabbing a handful of her hair, he played with it briefly before jerking her head back roughly. Lin Shi shrieked in fright and fell backwards on the bed with Chen Jiangshui landing right on top of her. She stopped screaming when she saw who it was. By then, Chen Jiangshui had already begun tearing off her pants. Suddenly realizing what was about to happen, Lin Shi began to struggle with all her might and yell at the top of her lungs. But all that seemed to do was make him more lustful than ever.

For Chen Jiangshui this was going to be a quick one. He was merely toying with Lin Shi, trying to humiliate her. Seeing a woman howling in pain beneath him gave him immense pleasure, as the satisfied glint in his eye and the mirthless laugh proved. He knew when he came inside her that it was a light ejaculation, but the pent-up feelings that had weighed heavily on his abdomen all morning, and whatever it was that had made his palms sweaty, seemed to have found instantaneous release. Feeling a pleasant lightness in his whole body, he fell into a sleep of extreme exhaustion.

The pain in the lower part of her body forced Lin Shi to prop herself up. A slight touch, and her hand came away with bright red blood. There were dark spots of blood, already congealed, on the blackish brown planks of the bed. Next to the spots of blood lay an even more menacing object—a shiny, long, sharp blade, Chen Jiangshui's butcher knife, which he had casually set down before climbing into bed.

Lin Shi crawled to the side of the bed, as far away from the knife as possible, and lay down again. Blood seemed to be still trickling down her legs. She didn't dare pull her pants back up, for fear of staining them. This time, she thought, she really was going to die. Overcome with exhaustion and weakness, she fell into a troubled sleep.

It was already noon when she was shaken awake. The sunlight streaming in through the room's tiny window hurt her eyes. Someone was standing in front of her holding a large bowl of rice. It wasn't until she had reached out to take it that she realized that the person was Chen Jiangshui.

Although it was leftover food from the previous night's wedding party, it included a large piece of fish; in her hunger, Lin Shi wolfed down the best meal she remembered ever having. It wasn't until she had finished that she noticed that Chen Jiangshui had been staring at her in a funny way. She looked down to discover that her pants were still down around her ankles. She had eaten this wonderful meal while she was naked from the waist down! Fearing that Chen Jiangshui would assault her again, and shocked by her own nudity, she hurriedly pulled up her pants and remained sitting on the bed, not daring to climb down. After looking at her a little longer, Chen Jiangshui said tersely that he was leaving and walked out the door.

Lin Shi sat on the bed until she was certain that he was not coming back. Then she swung one leg over the edge and climbed down, never imagining that just spreading her legs could cause such unbearable pain. She doubled over, clutching herself. The stuffed feeling was still there, but the tearing pain was already subsiding. After a while she managed to straighten up, but still she walked very gingerly, shuffling around the unfamiliar house with short, mincing steps. Although it was already noon, the rammed-earth house was dark and damp. The uneven earthen floor also gave off a cold, moist vapor. The lone double-paneled window was closed tightly, and a musty smell pervaded every corner of the place.

The entire house consisted only of a bedroom and a living area, separated by a curtain partition. A corner of the living area was equipped with a stove and functioned as the kitchen. It took Lin Shi no more than a few steps to make a complete circuit. At first she just walked around aimlessly, but when she saw how dirty and messy the place was, she found a bucket and some rags and began cleaning and scrubbing with the same diligence that had characterized her stay at her uncle's house.

After Lin Shi had been working for a while, she heard someone at the door. Assuming that it was Chen Jiangshui returning, she was about to rush off when a shrill female voice called out a greeting. Lin Shi responded and came out to see who her visitor was. The woman, who was in her fifties, had the typical dark skin of the fishing folks of Chencuo. Her face was deeply wrinkled and her snow-white hair was coiled into a bun at the back of her head. She had a brisk, no-nonsense look about her.

"I'm your next-door neighbor. Everyone calls me Auntie Ah-wang," the older woman said, displaying a full set of teeth, so gleaming white they looked more false than real.

Lin Shi shrank back and stood off to one side, lacking even the presence of mind to offer her guest a seat. This didn't bother Auntie Ah-wang, who glanced at the two rattan chairs, then sat down in the one by the door. Starting with her name and family, she asked Lin Shi about nearly everyone on her family tree before changing the subject and revealing in a low, conspiratorial whisper:

"Actually, I knew your mother."

Lin Shi slowly raised her head to look at Auntie Ah-wang, who had already switched to talking about Chen Jiangshui in a normal tone of voice. She was saying that he was a decent enough man, even though he wasn't in a very good line of work—killing pigs—and that when he ended up in the nether world, the pigs would be looking for revenge. There would be no escaping disembowelment, immersion in a pool of blood, and other such grim punishments, she predicted.

To hear her describe the scenes, one would have thought she had witnessed them herself, but her warning didn't have the hoped-for fearful effect on Lin Shi. Feeling a little put out, she took a different tack by inviting the younger woman to accompany her whenever she went to the Temple of the Chen Clan Elder. There Lin Shi could offer up sacrifices to expiate part of Chen Jiangshui's sins. Otherwise, in the nether world, where man and wife are considered equally guilty, she would have to bear part of the punishment.

Lin Shi's eyes widened with fear and she nodded a quick assent. Auntie Ah-wang was smiling as she uttered the Buddhist chant "Amitabha," for she had achieved her goal. Reaching into the pocket of her blue jacket, which was faded by countless washings, she groped around for a while before bringing out a piece of yellowish brown oil-paper. She opened it up with great care, revealing a round pat of black ointment.

"Here! There's nothing better for open wounds, if you know what I mean. Take it." She gave a knowing smile. A strange expression on her face made her appear shy and lecherous at the same time.

She was trying hard to look nonchalant, but with little success. "When I heard all those screams of yours last night and this morning," she said, "I kept chanting 'Amitabha' for you."

Lin Shi's cheeks reddened, and she lowered her head, too embarrassed to take the ointment.

"Go on, take it. What's there to be embarrassed about?"

Taking hold of Lin Shi's hand, Auntie Ah-wang forced the ointment into it.

"Didn't your aunt teach you anything?"

Lin Shi shook her head blankly.

"Ah, yes, a motherless child. You poor dear." Mumbling to herself, the older woman stood up.

"Got to go now," she said. "My fisherman will be back soon and he'll be hungry."

Lin Shi watched her leave, her eyes riveted on the woman's feet. Although once bound, they had subsequently been freed, which is why they weren't particularly small. Since there had never been any attempt to bind them into "three-inch golden lotuses," they were nearly as long as those of the average woman. The only difference was that she walked somewhat unsteadily, seemingly lifting her legs straight up, then setting them straight back down. She could only take small, mincing steps, and even those took a great deal of effort, so for her the simple act of walking was hard work.

Lin Shi sat there blankly, clutching the ointment in her hand, her eyes following Auntie Ah-wang as she veered off to the left and disappeared. The sky was gradually darkening. The pain down there had let up quite a bit by then. She had paid little attention to pain in recent years, preferring to just grit her teeth and bear it until it passed. But this feeling of being stuffed and stretched was hard to take, and she recalled the events of the previous night with alarm.

Tears began to course down her face. She wiped them away with the front of her jacket, but they quickly welled up again. She couldn't understand why the tears kept coming, since she didn't feel terribly sad. Surprised and bewildered, she sat there quietly, letting her tears flow, until she spotted Chen Jiangshui approaching in the distance.

At first she couldn't be sure that it was Chen Jiangshui. She knew only that it was a man out there, walking along the mudflats, and for the longest time he appeared to be making little headway in closing the distance. These mudflats actually extended all the way to the sea, but Lin Shi's view was blocked by patches of reeds and a few short trees, so that only a long strip of grayish yellow land was visible to her. The surface of this land, on which not a single blade of grass grew, was covered with pebbles. It was a barren and desolate landscape. In the evenings, with the enormous setting sun in the background and that breeze unique to Lucheng blowing in from the sea, stirring up a sky full of yellow sand, it was even more dreary and bleak.

In the orange glow of the setting sun, Lin Shi watched Chen Jiangshui approach. She was dimly aware that this was the man who was to be the mainstay of her life, or so people said. But just what did that mean? She wasn't sure. She could only watch her man making his way across the pebble-strewn grayish yellow land. At first he didn't seem to be making much headway, but by the time she could see him clearly, he was almost at the door.

As if by reflex, Lin Shi stood up to hide as Chen Jiangshui came striding into the house. He glanced at her as she cringed in the corner, then at the rearranged living room. "Haven't started dinner yet, hm?" he said without a trace of emotion. Then, flipping up the curtain, he went into the bedroom.

Lin Shi hurriedly fetched some straw from alongside the stove and started a fire. The familiar chore put her at ease, and when she lifted the lid of the pot to find it nearly half full of leftovers, she was more than relieved—she was almost happy.

She cooked some rice and heated up the leftovers. When she

heard Chen Jiangshui's returning footsteps, she quickly placed the pot of food on the bamboo table and picked up a bowl to fill it with rice. "Forget it!" he growled. Walking over to the bamboo cupboard against the wall, he took down a bottle of White Deer wine, snatched the ricebowl out of Lin Shi's hand, and filled it to the brim with wine. He took a big drink, tilting his head way back, then sat down with the bowl in his hand.

Again and again he filled then drained his bowl, occasionally picking up a morsel of food with his chopsticks. After a while it occurred to him that he was eating and drinking alone, while Lin Shi stood uncertainly off to the side.

"Aren't you going to eat?" he shouted, his spirits buoyed by the wine.

Lin Shi went into the kitchen, where she filled a large bowl with sweet-potato mash and rice. Caution demanded that she remain standing as she wolfed down her food in two or three swallows, washing it down with some soup from the bottom of the pot. Seeing that Chen Jiangshui was too engrossed in his drinking to pay any attention to her, she furtively refilled her bowl, taking care to press down hard on the rice. This time she ate at a more leisurely pace, first downing the sweet-potato mash, then savoring the nearly half-filled bowl of rice, chewing each bite slowly before swallowing it.

Although she wasn't exactly stuffed, she had had enough. Besides, filling the bowl again would be too risky, so she just leaned up against the stove. Before long, she had slid down until she was crouching on the floor against the stove. Feeling warm and cozy, she drifted off into a half sleep.

Chen Jiangshui continued drinking by himself, and after several bowls, even began humming a few bars of music. Now and then a song would form, and he'd sing a couple of lines:

As the second watch sounds, the moon lights up the courtyard;
I lead my darling girl into her chamber.
We are fated to be lovers tonight;
Pay no heed to what others say.

As he sang, he tapped his foot up and down, up and down, sometimes actually managing an accompanying rhythm to the music. Suddenly, he glanced down and saw that his bowl was empty. The lyrics died on his lips.

"Where the hell are you?" he bellowed. "Who do you think is going to pour the wine?"

Lin Shi woke with a start. Having had plenty of experience at being yelled at, she just pretended everything was fine. She got to her feet and, relying more on instinct than on anything else, moved toward Chen Jiangshui to await his orders.

"Come on, you slut! Join me!" He wrapped his arms around her waist.

Too late Lin Shi realized why he had called her, and now there was no escape. Out of fear she picked up the bottle and docilely filled his bowl.

"Drink! Drink up!" Chen Jiangshui's speech was getting slurred.

Lin Shi took the wine and tried a sip. In winters past she had sometimes sneaked a little wine to help ward off the cold—on many a day it had been all that kept her from freezing to death. If she'd been able to handle home brew made from milky-white glutinous rice, which had made her choke with nearly every mouthful, then this distilled wine ought to be child's play.

When Chen Jiangshui saw Lin Shi down the wine with ease, his original enthusiasm rapidly waned. "Go on, get out of my sight!" he barked, swatting her with a backward fling of his hand that sent her reeling.

Chen Jiangshui laughed with delight as Lin Shi lost her balance and sat down hard on the floor. He dug out a few copper coins and threw them at her.

"I won today, so here's some 'opening night' money for my favorite slut."

Lin Shi crept back over to the stove and crouched, terrified, beside it. She didn't dare to go over and pick up the scattered coins, and going back to sleep was out of the question, so she just leaned her face against the red bricks. Whether it was because of the wine or the lateness of the hour, she didn't know, but the warm feeling from the stove gradually dissipated, leaving only a faint trace of warmth on her cheeks.

Lin Shi apparently forgotten, Chen Jiangshui tilted his head back to drain the last drops of wine from the bowl and belched loudly. Without so much as a glance at her, he got to his feet, staggered into the bedroom, and before long was snoring loudly.

Lin Shi huddled by the stove, still too frightened to move. Her attention focused on the rhythmic rise and fall of Chen Jiangshui's snoring, she heard the volume gradually even out. At its peak, his breath came out in a loud *whoosh,* as though untold injustices suffered over thousands of years all needed to find release at the same instant. She listened for a while longer, making certain that he was sound asleep. Then, crawling on all fours, she crept away from the stove and searched carefully for the copper coins scattered over the floor.

Outside, night had already fallen; inside, a five-watt light bulb gave off a dim light. Unable to see clearly, Lin Shi groped around, relying on memory and touch. She quickly gathered up a few coins, which were nearly the same color as the dirt floor. Not ready to give up yet, she looked around some more, but when she was satisfied that she had found them all, she squatted on the floor and counted them.

There was one thick "good" coin and three thin "bad" ones.
She was overjoyed. Her first thought was to find something to
wrap them in, but there was nothing. Reaching into the pocket
of her jacket, she felt the ointment that Auntie Ah-wang had left
with her that afternoon. She held it in her palm and examined it.
Of course: The square piece of oil-paper it was wrapped in was
just the right size. She wasted no time in scraping out the ointment and replacing it with the four small copper coins, not caring that they became smeared with ointment. Then she wrapped
them up tightly and pocketed the tiny bundle.

Her treasure safely tucked away, Lin Shi heaved a sigh of relief
and sat down. Just then she spotted a dab of ointment on her
index finger. Remembering what Auntie Ah-wang had said, she
pulled down her underpants and, in the dim light, smeared the
ointment all over the area between her legs. It had a special cool-
ness that felt nice when she put it on, and the black color was sure
to make it look repulsive. It was just what Lin Shi needed, for
now, even though she got dressed without putting her underpants on, she felt well protected.

The next order of business—washing and putting away the
dishes—took her hardly any time. She dried her hands, then
looked around for something else to do. The wind was howling
outside, whirling and turning, occasionally making a hissing
sound as though it were breaking out of an encirclement. Growing a little frightened, Lin Shi tiptoed softly over to the bedroom doorway, lifted the curtain, and peeked inside. Chen Jiangshui was fast asleep, his arms and legs all spread out. After staring
at him for a while, she timidly entered the room and lay down
fully clothed in the corner closest to the door. She had no sooner
closed her eyes than she heard Chen Jiangshui turn over and
mumble something. She sat bolt upright, hugging tightly to herself the bundle she had brought over from her uncle's house, all

set to rush out the door. But he had only been tossing in his sleep and soon settled back down.

Lin Shi was too jumpy to lie down again, so she leaned against the wall beside the bed. The bundle clutched tightly in her arms, she drifted off to sleep.

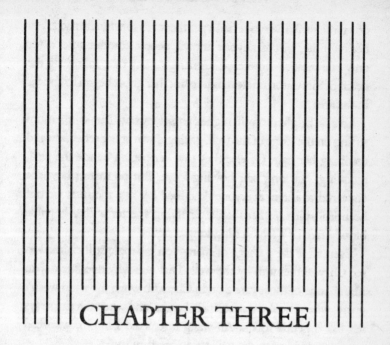

CHAPTER THREE

In the center of Chencuo, to the right and behind the Temple of the Chen Clan Elder, was a well that had always been the subject of strange stories. Its round opening was encircled by an octagonal wall about three or four feet off the ground. Time and exposure to the elements had turned the bright red bricks of the wall into a water-soaked, dull red. Moist green moss flourished at the base of the well, which was slick and dank. The ledge, worn smooth and shiny from frequent use, was extremely slippery. When it was wet, people had to be especially careful not to lean too far over the edge, or they might fall head over heels into the well.

The most recent and popular story going around concerned a servant girl named Chrysanthemum, who had thrown herself down the well. Everyone had a pet theory as to why she had taken her own life, but as anyone knows, people commit suicide for only one reason—to escape torment. At any rate, following the death of this unfortunate maidservant, her ghost began to appear in the area.

Late on bright moonlit nights, passersby saw Chrysanthemum sitting on the ledge of the well, gazing down at her reflection and combing her hair. Or else they saw her pacing beside the well, moaning, her long hair flowing loose. But no matter how she appeared to them, everyone described her as a melancholic but beautiful spirit, rather than a terrifying specter with a horrible bloody face or a frightening long tongue.

Even after the passage of many years, people still claimed to see Chrysanthemum by the well. That was why one fine day in March, one of those rare days in Chencuo when the wind wasn't gusty, when the sky was serenely bright, and when the sun's rays felt like a gentle touch, Ah-wang instructed Lin Shi, who had accompanied her to the well to do her laundry:

"Since the well is right next to the Temple of the Elder, it's under the administration of the Elder himself. Even ghosts can appear around here. Which shows how kind and powerful the Elder is. He gives people who have suffered injustices a chance to have their say."

As Lin Shi, who was holding a washboard and a basketful of laundry, listened to the old woman, she began to look around her. There among the banyan trees she spotted a corner of the temple, its swallowtail edge curving upwards to form a sweeping arch that reached up into the boundless, clear blue sky. A light breeze, with wispy white clouds in tow, drifted softly by.

"That's right," thought Lin Shi. "The Elder lets the ghosts appear and air their grievances."

Lin Shi truly believed that the ghost, by making her presence felt, finally had her grievances redressed. Filled with fearful reverence, she placed her washboard and laundry basket in a corner beside the well, then gazed down into the bottomless well.

"Chrysanthemum," she prayed silently as she drew up some water, "let your spirit be my protector!"

She looked around self-consciously at the women washing their clothes by the well and was relieved to see that no one was paying any attention. She picked up the bucket of water and walked quickly to her laundry basket.

Although it was already eight or nine o'clock, the well wasn't particularly crowded that morning. The women who had to get up early to go into the fields or out to sea had done their laundry at the break of dawn, so nearly all those who came at this hour were older women who were helping the working women or were washing some of their own personal items. Those few who took in washing from other families would still be at the well at noon.

The area within a seven- or eight-foot radius of the well was paved with gray speckled stones, and today, even though there weren't many women around, it was covered with piles of laundry, washboards, and buckets. Following a whole morning of laundry runoff, the drainage ditch wasn't functioning very well. It had been designed to carry the dirty water off to a trough, which fed a nearby irrigation ditch; but it was already becoming clogged, and assorted cast-off objects lay soaking in the puddles—a pair of torn underpants here, a pair of worn-out wooden clogs there—all bloated and giving off the dank marshy smell of stagnant water. So even under the blue sky of such a warm spring day, there was a feeling of oppressive closeness.

The women by the well, most of whom were getting on in years, all wore old clothes in dark, dull colors while they worked. Heads down and teeth clenched, they either scrubbed hard at their wash or pounded noisily with their laundry mallets. Now and then, one or two children playing nearby would stray too close and get ordered off with loud curses. Not that the women demanded quiet, for they frequently exchanged whispers, passing on the latest bit of gossip and giggling softly. They were always on the alert, ready to soak up any news that came their way, for missing even the slightest tidbit could result in a loss of face.

The high point of the day was reached with the arrival of one or two of the older women—the resident moralists. The other women would listen to them raptly, occasionally whispering and laughing among themselves, passing on comments that the older women had let slip and adding their own opinions. Once in a while, when the gossip was particularly juicy, they would all be giggling so much they'd have to stop what they were doing.

Auntie Ah-wang was commonly recognized as being one of those women who livened things up wherever she went. She was anything but a shrinking violet. Once, for example, she had snatched a pair of pants stained with menstrual blood right out of another woman's hands and, after waving them in the air for all to see, said contemptuously: "How could any self-respecting girl put something like this in the wash for her sister-in-law to see? What kind of a girl would do that?"

Auntie Ah-wang seemed to know who was doing the washing for whom in every single family. Once she saw a washerwoman standing near her washing a pair of men's underpants with bloodstains on them; her pronounced moral verdict was accompanied by a meaningful shake of her head: "Now how do you suppose he got this? I see he still hasn't learned self-control. His mother has to be told."

"For something like this," someone interjected with a laugh, "wouldn't it be better to tell his wife?"

"What the hell good would that do?" Auntie Ah-wang said

scornfully. She quickly answered her own question: "If it was his wife who got him into this mess, or if she was the type who could control him, he wouldn't have sent out a pair of underpants like this for us to wash in the first place."

There were knowing chuckles all around.

Most of the time Lin Shi laughed along with the others, even though she never quite understood what they were laughing at. She didn't mind fetching water for Auntie Ah-wang, for it was she, after all, who had brought her to the well in the first place; besides, Lin Shi was so much quicker and stronger than the older woman. Sometimes, when Auntie Ah-wang was still busily holding forth after Lin Shi had finished her own laundry, she would unobtrusively finish the other woman's laundry for her as well. Ah-wang usually pretended not to notice, continuing to talk until she came to a break in her monologue, giving Lin Shi plenty of time to finish the washing. Then she'd exclaim, as though taken completely by surprise: "You have such a good heart, you'll surely be rewarded. Kindness is always rewarded."

Then she would tell Lin Shi how fortunate she was: no parents-in-law to lord it over her, no brothers- or sisters-in-law to care for, and no need to work in the fields or go to sea—all she had to do was see to the daily needs of two people.

"That kind of good fortune comes only after generations of virtuous cultivation," Auntie Ah-wang once said emphatically.

Lin Shi kept her head down and remained silent, but the hint of a smile appeared on her long face, which had grown ruddier of late. She self-consciously straightened the front of her jacket, for it had grown tight from a very noticeable development of her figure—even her undershirt was exposed.

Lin Shi had filled out a lot more than one would expect in the short six months she had been married. It was as though the development that had been denied her before was now making up for lost time. Not only did her arms suddenly flesh out, but unmistakable feminine signs also began to manifest themselves. She had always been a tall, long-faced girl. Her single-lidded, almond-shaped eyes had lately taken on a misty look. People who saw her these days had nothing but nice things to say about her appearance. They would never have guessed that someone who had once been as flat as a board could turn into such an attractive young woman.

Auntie Ah-wang eyed Lin Shi coolly, observing how a few words of praise could produce such a pleased look on her face. She also noticed, when Lin Shi bent over, how her jacket stretched tightly across her bosom. An icy comment escaped from her thin, compressed lips and two rows of perfect white teeth: "Fate's been good to you. How can a widow like me even hope to compare? Too bad for me—I must have some unpaid debts from a former life."

Lowering her voice and leaning so close to Lin Shi that she could have bitten her ear, she added in a confidential tone: "That man of yours, once he mounts you he just goes crazy. Every time I hear you scream, I start chanting 'Amitabha.'"

The look of pity remained on Auntie Ah-wang's face after she had said her piece, but almost immediately she made a sign with her eyes to the circle of women listening eagerly, and pouted in Lin Shi's direction. The women who were nearest looked at Lin Shi knowingly, with a mixture of pity and scorn.

Lin Shi reined in her smile. Dejected, she lowered her head and absentmindedly resumed her scrubbing, forcing herself to become oblivious to what was going on around her.

Auntie Ah-wang kept her eye on Lin Shi, who kept her head lowered for the longest time. She kept scrubbing one of Auntie Ah-wang's old shirts, somehow managing to miss completely the large soy-sauce stain on the front. Concerned that Lin Shi might

not get it clean even if she worked at it all morning, the old woman said loudly: "That's why I say the only way to expiate the sins
of a former life is to believe in the Guanyin Bodhisattva. And I
don't mean just not eating meat on the first day of the month,
then letting it slide for three or four months. Or going over to the
temple on the fifteenth of the month, if you happen to think of it,
and offering some sacrifices. No, you have to have Guanyin in
your heart at all times."

Auntie Ah-wang said this in such a comical way that the wom-
en standing nearby all started laughing. Lin Shi joined in the
laughter. As she raised her head, her gaze again fell on the corner
of the temple roof, with its carvings of crouching dragons and
phoenixes. In the morning light, the temple eaves, which seemed
to be resting on the hilltop, shone with a yellow gleam. All was
peaceful and serene, except for the green enamel dragon crouching on the swallowtail ridge under the blue sky, seemingly poised
for flight. Lin Shi murmured a silent "Amitabha" and, lowering
her head once more, continued washing the shirt that she had
been holding in her hands.

A shrill voice rose to take over for Auntie Ah-wang. Lin Shi
looked up quickly. It was the middle-aged widow Spring Bough,
who lived with her only son in the lane behind the well. She was a
small woman with a voice so high-pitched she seemed to be constantly pinching her throat to speak in falsetto. Lin Shi recalled
Auntie Ah-wang's telling her once that Spring Bough's voice was
a sort of "blemish," which, as it turned out, was the main reason
she had ended up a widow.

"Did you all know . . . ?"

She always started off like that, pausing briefly to scan the
crowd, just in case someone objectionable was there, before going on. Many a pair of curious ears had been lured by that well-
timed pause.

"My neighbor, Ah-qian's mother . . . well, her Ah-qian has been fooling around so long it isn't news anymore. But, did you know that she recently decided it was time to get him a wife, so she went to see a family in Beijiaotou to try to make a match?"

"I know," quickly volunteered a woman by the name of Wang-shi. "It was Meiguan's daughter. The matchmaker is a relative of my fifth aunt." She was immensely pleased with herself for being so well-informed. Her husband, a well-known fisherman in Chen-cuo, was equally well-known for losing every argument he had with her.

"That's right!" Buoyed by the unanticipated collaboration, Spring Bough's spirits rose even higher. "Well, at that meeting the two families got on like they were made for each other. Then when the deal was just about set, Ah-qian's mother took the young lady's hand and started talking a blue streak, eventually getting around to the subject of Ah-qian."

Spring Bough paused to take a breather. The women around her clamored for her to go on.

"Okay, hold your horses. I'll get to it." She was being deliberately coy. "Do you know what Ah-qian's mother said? She told them that her son was always fooling around with women, that he treated his home like a hotel, and that he spent every penny he made on those sluts of his. He'd fetch water for them to bathe their feet and even wash their underwear for them . . . "

"You don't say!" a voice in the crowd gasped.

The others merely laughed.

"What happened after that?" Wangshi asked.

"She scared that young lady half to death, that's what! And the poor girl hadn't even crossed the threshold yet. And you know what else? Ah-qian's mother started weeping and sniffling, whining about how she had brought her son up all by herself and how she expected her daughter-in-law to be good to her."

"What a fool!"

"What does she use for brains?"

The comments flew.

"But what about the marriage?" Wangshi persisted.

"Oh, I'm sure it's been called off," Spring Bough said indifferently. "With a mother-in-law like that, who wouldn't want to run and hide?"

Since these recent developments were news to her, Wangshi was feeling a bit put out.

"I didn't hear my fifth aunt mention any of this." She sounded like a woman who wasn't going to rest until she had gotten to the bottom of things.

"I'll ask her the next time I see her."

Suddenly someone cut in coldly: "Who's to say that Ah-qian's mother didn't do it on purpose?"

Everyone turned. It was Auntie Ah-wang, who had been silent for some time. She continued in a flat, emotionless voice:

"That way she could teach them a lesson, show them that this was one mother-in-law who had a couple of cards up her sleeve."

Obviously this had occurred to no one else, and a momentary silence set in. Then the oldest woman among them, Grandmother Gu, who still had a husband, sons, and grandsons around her, coughed to clear her throat; with a tolerance that came from maturity, she said calmly and gently: "Ah-wang, it's not that I enjoy picking on you, but only you would come up with something like that about people. You've got a wicked tongue when it comes to talking about others. Just like a knife."

Auntie Ah-wang responded with a soft "Hmph!" but said nothing. Seeing the expression on Auntie Ah-wang's face, Grandmother Gu just smiled and dropped the matter.

For a while they all quietly busied themselves with their laundry. But before long the sound of hushed whispers was heard again, followed by a sudden outburst from Wangshi: "What? You actually think people like that would give their daughter a dowry? Why, when their first grandson was a month old, all they sent over was some sticky rice—not even a small piece of green onion or a slice of meat."

At first the women just giggled, but they wasted little time in pursuing the question of which family she was talking about.

Lin Shi listened in silence. When the other women laughed, she laughed along with them. Their conversation was a continuous source of amazement to her. Before, when she was living in her uncle's house, there had been eight cousins to take care of, not to mention an invalid aunt, who had somehow managed to have one child after another even though she was laid up in bed the year round. All Lin Shi had ever been exposed to was work, seemingly unending work. On top of it all, there was the war, to which every family responded by bolting its doors as soon as night fell. So Lin Shi, who hardly ever got a chance to talk to other people, was ignorant of what was going on around her. On the rare occasions she chanced to hear a bit of news in those days, she found she wasn't the least bit interested.

When she met Auntie Ah-wang, a new world opened up to her, making her aware, as though for the first time, of people and events she had never noticed before. Unfortunately, she still hadn't met most of the people who were being talked about— that would make it a lot more interesting, she thought. She also cherished the vague hope that someday she could participate knowledgeably in the discussions, like the rest of the women, telling stories about this person and that, maybe even contributing a comment from time to time.

The women gossiped with such fervor that morning that Lin Shi stayed later than she should have, not getting home until after ten o'clock. As soon as she walked in the front door and saw Chen Jiangshui sitting in the rattan chair in the living room, she knew she was in for it. Her fears were borne out the moment he laid eyes on her.

"Where the hell have you been?" he snarled.

She recoiled, shifting the clothes in the laundry basket she was holding at her waist.

"Since when does it take all morning just to wash a few things? If you like washing so much, I'll take in some laundry for you. So much it'll take you a year to finish!" he growled angrily.

"It was more crowded than usual today," she explained timidly.

Chen Jiangshui leapt out of the chair, lunged forward, and slapped her across the mouth.

"Fuck your old mother! How dare you talk back to me!"

Lin Shi rubbed her red, swollen cheek and lowered her head. But Chen Jiangshui wasn't finished with her yet: "I know damned well you've been hanging around with that old slut Ah-wang again. Well, screw her old mother, too! If I catch you gossiping with her anymore, I'll cut out your tongue with my butcher knife!"

He sounded like he meant every word he said—no idle threats there—and Lin Shi was trembling with fear. Then she saw his hand moving toward her breast, and even though she knew what he wanted, she couldn't help screaming.

He had already set a pattern of wanting her when he returned from the slaughterhouse in the morning. The only question was how often. During the "honeymoon" period she had been forced to endure her man nearly every other day. Occasionally, the intervals were even shorter, and he might want her several times in a single day. Always he would reach for her when she was least prepared. Whether she had a fire going in the stove or an armful of laundry ready to hang up to dry, he simply didn't care. And it invariably led to repeated screams from her.

She resisted him, instinctively, but she was no match for his strength. In the end she would be pinned beneath him, watching his greasy face drawing nearer and nearer, watching the narrow eyes buried deep in flabby flesh gleam with a bestial light.

He still hurt her every time. In the darkness of the room, she had no way of knowing exactly what he was doing to her, and her ingrained modesty kept her from opening her eyes to see his actual movements. She knew only that he filled her up down there, that his weight pressing down on her made her gasp for breath, that the pain would be so unbearable she could only scream and moan.

Blessedly, no matter how much or how little time it took him, it always came to an end. He would roll off her, stretch out on the bed, and fall asleep immediately, snoring loudly. For Lin Shi, the most unendurable part of the day had passed, and by the time she got up and straightened her clothes, the pain had already begun to subside. Past experience told her that it would soon go away altogether, as long as Chen Jiangshui didn't assault her again right away.

And so, an almost happy Lin Shi walked out of the room and went over to the stove. It was already an established routine. On the days that Chen Jiangshui wanted her, he would come home with fish, oysters, and, now and then, some meat. And on special occasions there might even be viscera, like liver and heart. Lin Shi carefully examined the food left on the stove today, then returned to the living room feeling pretty satisfied. She picked up the basket of wet laundry and went outside.

A March day in Lucheng, not a breath of wind. The heavens,

incomparably bright and beautiful, an even blue stretching to the edge of the sky. There, where the sea meets the sky, patches of reeds grow on the mudflats, new shoots forming eye-catching patches of fresh green. The sun's rays so gentle they cannot dispel the lingering spring chill that brushes the face.

Lin Shi quickly hung out the clothes on the bamboo pole. With a light heart, she went back into the house to prepare lunch. Suddenly realizing that she had forgotten to bring the laundry basket in with her, she turned and stepped out the door just as someone stumbled out from the corner of the low earthen wall next door. It was Auntie Ah-wang.

Lin Shi was caught totally by surprise. Auntie Ah-wang gave the appearance of having crouched at the base of the wall for some time, for she could barely straighten up. When she saw Lin Shi, her face screwed itself up into a smile, a very strange smile. Her eyes were suspiciously bright as she gave the younger woman a searching look. Inexplicably, Lin Shi was reminded of the look in Chen Jiangshui's eyes whenever he drew near her.

"I think this wall's about to fall down. I was just propping it up a little."

Auntie Ah-wang was clearly embarrassed. Spring sunshine gave her face a rosy glow.

"But it's all right now. Well, I have to go get lunch ready."

Without waiting for Lin Shi to say anything, she turned on her heel and limped across the courtyard and into her own house as quickly as her once-bound feet would allow. Lin Shi glanced at the wall, which seemed sturdy enough to her, but she still had to prepare lunch, too, so she went inside, forgetting all about Ah-wang's odd behavior.

There was fish and meat for lunch, which Lin Shi threw into the pot, adding some soy sauce and making a three-layered stew.

As usual, there was so much soy sauce that the meat almost tasted pickled. Lunch was ready, but Chen Jiangshui was still asleep. Lin Shi decided to sample the stew, and she didn't stop until the salt forced her to put down her chopsticks.

Chen Jiangshui slept later than usual that day, not getting out of bed until nearly one o'clock. Looking rested and in good humor, he wolfed down his lunch in silence, then left without saying a word, walking briskly in the direction of the reed patches on the mudflats. As she watched his figure disappear into the distance, Lin Shi began listlessly to clear the table.

After washing up, she yawned. Since there was nothing else to do, she went into the bedroom and lay down. She soon fell fast asleep. Normally she would sleep for two or three hours, then get up to prepare dinner before Chen Jiangshui returned. But that afternoon, perhaps because she had eaten so much salty pork, she had one dream after another, finally waking up with a terrible thirst. In her dreams she was mixing sweet-potato mash and rice with salt. There was nothing else to eat, and the salt finally got the better of her. She reached into her mouth and scratched— blood came gushing out. When she sucked on the blood, it too was salty.

Lin Shi got out of bed and went into the other room for some water. Outside, the dazzling afternoon sun shone. With a start, she realized the significance of the situation. She, of all people, had had the good fortune to take a real nap in broad daylight.

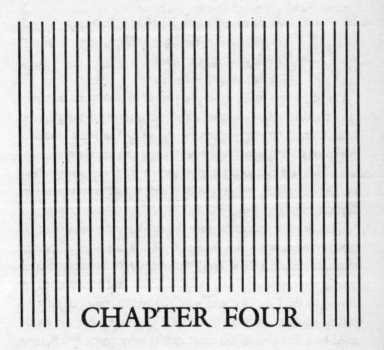

CHAPTER FOUR

With her daily undisturbed afternoon naps, Lin Shi's days fairly flew by. It seemed like only yesterday that the oysters had been planted during the fifth month, and here it was already time for the Dead Souls' Festival.

Lucheng had a long and involved series of rites for the dead that began on the first day of the seventh month and continued through the second day of the following month, with each district taking a turn in offering sacrifices. To make it easier for people to remember, the schedule had been made into a ditty, which went like this:

> *On the first, let go the river lanterns;*
> *On the second, sacrifices at the Palace;*

On the third, Rice Market Street;

. . . .

On the twenty-ninth, it's Harbor District;
On the thirtieth, the Street of Shops;
On the first, Beggar Town;
On the second, Noodle Town.

This ditty was such an integral part of local custom that even small children could recite it easily from memory. So during the seventh lunar month, the inhabitants of each district observed their turn according to the rhyme. On the appointed day a sumptuous feast was prepared for all the orphaned spirits and wandering ghosts, which, the people believed, would ensure peace in their district.

When it came to sacrifices for the dead, the people spared no expense. Sometimes the lavishness of the offerings surpassed even those made at New Year's. In addition to a charitable concern for the orphaned, homeless ghosts who had been cooped up all year by the City God and were allowed to come out only on this occasion to enjoy the sacrifices, the people were also motivated by a fear that unless these ghosts were properly fed, they might entrench themselves in the area and make trouble.

And so one afternoon during the seventh month of that year, as the Dead Souls' Festival drew near, Lin Shi was roused from a deep sleep by someone calling her name. Swaying on her once-bound feet, Auntie Ah-wang came into the house, and after repeated calls failed to rouse Lin Shi, she raised her voice and called out in half-serious alarm: "What, are you napping again? You youngsters sure don't know how to appreciate the treasure of your youth. The idea! Sleeping in broad daylight! Aren't you afraid of cutting your life short?"

Lin Shi rushed out of the room, feeling the awkwardness of the situation, but trying to worm her way out of it somehow.

"I wasn't really sleeping. Just resting my eyes. There's nothing much to do, anyhow."

"You lazybones!" Auntie Ah-wang chided her gently. "Even at my age I don't dare lie down for an afternoon nap. I'm afraid I might never wake up."

"Oh no, oh no." That's all Lin Shi, who wasn't very good at defending herself, could say.

"But I didn't come over here to lecture you. I want to remind you that the Dead Souls' Festival is coming up. Here in Chencuo we observe the seventeenth as our day of sacrifice, not the twenty-seventh, as you did back in Anping. Now remember: Old Palace District observes the fifteenth, Eastrock the sixteenth, and Chencuo the seventeenth. We're expected to offer our sacrifices on the seventeenth."

Although she insisted she hadn't come over just to pass the time of day, Auntie Ah-wang sat around talking until the sun was well into the western sky before she got up and rushed home.

Lin Shi was infected by Auntie Ah-wang's enthusiasm over the coming festival, and as soon as Chen Jiangshui came home that evening, she asked him anxiously what they were expected to do. The casualness of his response surprised her:

"I'll take care of everything at the proper time. We're not like those fishing folk who have to make peace with the orphaned, homeless spirits to ensure their own safety at sea."

Lin Shi was still not convinced, so he added: "Don't you worry. When it comes to offering sacrifices, I put on a pretty good show."

So Lin Shi set her mind at ease. She had been worried that her pig-butcher husband wouldn't even take part in the Dead Souls' Festival and that half of the calamities would befall her, just as Auntie Ah-wang had said. But now, while all her Chencuo neighbors were busy with their preparations, Lin Shi still had time to take her daily naps. Sometimes she would wake up early, when the afternoon sun was still shining brightly, and wonder how she could afford to sleep in broad daylight during this busy month. This gave her an uneasy feeling, and her only consolation was the thought, "Maybe this is what Auntie Ah-wang meant by a 'blessed' life."

If not for Chen Jiangshui's persistent demands on her, Lin Shi would have readily believed that she truly was "blessed." Chen Jiangshui still took her whenever he felt like it, and once he became aware that she had gotten used to the way he was mistreating her, and that her screams had lessened a little, he stepped up his abuses. After one particularly violent bout, Lin Shi discovered bruises all over her arms, and they took more than ten days to disappear.

Auntie Ah-wang came over for a visit that afternoon. Lin Shi's shirt-sleeves reached all the way down to her elbows, as was the prevailing fashion, even though it was the middle of summer. Still, they weren't long enough to cover up the dark splotches on her arms. Auntie Ah-wang glanced at them and said solemnly: "Even though we're friends and neighbors, I'm not sure I should say this to you . . ."

She looked at Lin Shi, coyly hesitant. Lin Shi stared back at her uncomprehendingly. Finally, the urge to speak got the better of her, and the words tumbled out swiftly:

"You know the seventh month belongs to the dead, so a baby conceived during this month is the reincarnation of a dead soul. The elements in the baby's horoscope will vie with each other, ensuring a life of toil and trouble. Now, the last thing you want is a demonic pregnancy like that, so how can you be so ignorant—how can you continue, during this month, to . . ."

These fearful words had the desired effect on Lin Shi, who quickly voiced her anguish:

"I'm not the one who wants it. What can I do?"

Auntie Ah-wang laughed.

"What a simpleton! At times like this, you . . . all you have to do is fake it."

"What do you mean, fake it?"

"Tell him you're having an unusually long period this month. Keep it up long enough and before you know it, the month will be over."

"Sure, why not?" Lin Shi said joyfully. Realizing that it might work, her face lit up.

The two women talked the afternoon away, with Auntie Ah-wang eagerly gossiping about their neighbors. Unlike previous days, she was in no hurry to go home to prepare dinner and continued sitting until the sun was low in the western sky. She started complaining about her daughter-in-law. By now, Lin Shi was used to hearing Auntie Ah-wang object to her daughter-in-law's arrogance. Time and again she had heard how the young woman refused to defer to her mother-in-law and how, because she helped take care of a few oyster beds, she acted like the livelihood of the entire family depended on her.

"I still have a son I can depend on. I don't need to eat a single mouthful of that woman's rice," Auntie Ah-wang said resolutely. "That son of mine, I raised him all by myself from the age of three. His father—that damned old man—went out fishing one day and came back in a box. He was so bloated we couldn't even get a shroud on him."

At first Lin Shi was just listening absentmindedly, volunteering a word or two now and then. After all, she had heard the story more times than she could remember. Yet when the older woman reached this point, Lin Shi felt sorry for her and wanted to say something comforting. But she didn't know where to begin, so she just sat with her mouth shut, giving Auntie Ah-wang her undivided attention.

The sun began its gradual descent in the west, setting the dis-

THE BUTCHER'S WIFE

tant sky aglow with brilliant, intoxicating red hues. The weather was always like this—hot and dry—in the middle of summer. Usually sunlight filled the vast, cloudless sky, but at that moment, clouds had appeared from out of nowhere, gathering to form a dusty gray expanse where the sea met the sky. As the sea of clouds swallowed up the sun, they burst into a golden red, as though they had caught fire. They began to transform themselves into myriad shapes. Over there, a vicious lion; over here, a lotus, crowned with layers of red petals. One after another the shapes came, all of them bathed in the same golden light, all of them incredibly bright and beautiful.

Even the tips of the distant reeds had a golden red tint. Now that it was midsummer, the reeds had turned dark green, standing tall in patches here and there and swaying gracefully in the wind. In between the patches, fishing folk in groups of twos and threes could be seen pushing two-wheeled carts filled with their harvests of oysters, heading toward town with their catch. With the sun at their backs, their long shadows stretched ahead of them, arriving at their destination long before they did.

One group after another passed by. Most were quite young, especially the women, many of whom had small children who rode on the carts. The men, on the other hand, varied in age. Apart from the suntanned, muscular youngsters, there were a few oldsters whose hair and goatees were streaked with gray and whose bodies were hunched over like wind-dried shrimp.

Even though they were obviously quite weary, the fishing folk all walked with firm, steady steps. As they passed beneath the banyan tree in front of the house where Auntie Ah-wang and Lin Shi were sitting, they called out friendly greetings:

"Sitting outside, are you?"

"We're on our way home."

Auntie Ah-wang sat there, perfectly composed, returning

each greeting until she saw her daughter-in-law, Harmony, approaching. Then she purposefully turned her head away and discussed at length, and in the most sarcastic tones possible, her daughter-in-law's insufferable arrogance. Apparently concerned that the others might not be able to hear her, she even raised her voice a level or two.

Auntie Ah-wang's daughter-in-law was a short, heavyset woman with a full but compact figure. With the sun behind her, she looked even more solid than usual as she drew near. She had taken off her bamboo hat, revealing in the fading light a tanned, round face with regular features, marred perhaps by the wrinkles between her brows. Gravitating toward the ridge of her nose, these wrinkles were a natural result of constant squinting before the wind. There was no doubt that she was aware of Auntie Ah-wang's presence beneath the banyan tree, yet she walked right past without so much as a word, as though she hadn't seen her at all.

Auntie Ah-wang prattled on and on until this particular group of fishing folk had moved on down the road, then rose and sauntered homeward on her once-bound feet.

Lin Shi went home to start the rice for dinner. Just then she heard a string of screams and curses from Auntie Ah-wang and an occasional response from her deep-voiced daughter-in-law. Harmony spoke slowly but had a big voice, and she more than made up for her lack of verbal speed with a deep sonority and superior staying power. Auntie Ah-wang, on the other hand, found that after letting loose a shrill volley of abuses, she was gasping for air and was forced to slow down, while her daughter-in-law continued at her original speed without missing a beat. All in all, they seemed to be evenly matched as they traded curses.

Suddenly, the unmistakable sound of a loud slap rent the air. Harmony came running out of the house, holding her cheek and wailing pitifully. Auntie Ah-wang was hot on her heels, a broom in her hand, its long handle waving menacingly in the air. It was about all she could do just to keep going on those unbound feet of hers, but she found the energy to curse as she ran:

"All right, fine! You go ahead and run outside! I'll tell the whole neighborhood about you, you stinking whore! I slave at home every day, cooking your meals for you. The only thing I don't do is spoon-feed you, but are you satisfied? No, not you! And if I complain about you, all you do is talk back. If I didn't beat you, you'd get on your high horse and never come down!"

"Don't you get the idea I'm scared of you!" Harmony railed as she ran away from the older woman. "If you weren't too old to stand a beating, I'd show you."

The chase didn't last long. The daughter-in-law, with youth and strength on her side, soon left Auntie Ah-wang far behind. As Harmony watched the older woman's limping gait grow increasingly pronounced (a sure sign that she would never catch up), she stood in the doorway and had her say, like someone who had all the time in the world:

"Who says you're supplying my food? I suppose you think I go out to the oyster beds every day just for show! If it weren't for you, you old hag, with all your handouts, I'd already have everything I ever wanted—good food, clothes, everything!"

"What's that! How dare you say that! I dare you to say that again!" Shaking with rage, Auntie Ah-wang lit out after her daughter-in-law, her gray hair tumbling down in front of her face and making her look very much like a mad old woman.

"You're damned right I'll say it again! I'll tell everybody . . ."

Before Harmony even had a chance to finish, Auntie Ah-wang caught her off guard by hurling the broom at her with all her might. As it whizzed past her ear, she shrieked, "Help! Murder!" then darted into the house, slamming the double doors behind her and bolting them shut. By the time Auntie Ah-wang retrieved her weapon—the broom—it was too late. She tried banging frantically on the door with the broom, but to no avail. Then she dashed around to the back, but Harmony had already locked the kitchen door. Once the realization that she was locked out of her own house sunk in, Auntie Ah-wang walked back, the broom in her hand dragging uselessly on the ground behind her, and began hurling curses toward the inside of the house:

"You're going to die an early death, you cunt! You've got no conscience, you cunt! You think lightning won't strike you down, huh? You think you can lock me out of my own house, huh? Well, if you had any guts, you'd come out here instead of hiding behind a locked door."

"Well, if you're so clever, find a way to get in here. If you do, you can beat me any way you like," Harmony goaded her.

Auntie Ah-wang screamed and cursed for all she was worth, but her daughter-in-law refused to open the door. By then their shouts had attracted a crowd of curious neighbors, and the sight of all those people, plus the realization that there was nothing she could do about being locked out of her house by her own daughter-in-law, made her painfully aware that she was rapidly losing face. Like a woman who has taken leave of her senses, she began pounding furiously on the door with her broom. Then she hurled her skinny frame against the door like a battering ram—a shaky one, to be sure—never letting up with her curses, even though she was gasping for breath: "You crazy cunt! Used-up cunt! An old cunt used up by a thousand—no, ten thousand— men! Up your old lady's cunt! You shameless, stinking cunt!"

"Leave my mother out of it—she's a decent, chaste woman. And you don't have to keep calling me cunt-this, cunt-that. After all, I am *your* daughter-in-law, and if I've been screwed by thousands—no, tens of thousands—of men, it's not exactly something for you to crow about!"

She then raised her voice even louder as she went on the offensive: "Everybody knows it's your cunt that needs fucking! Everybody knows just what kind of widow's life you've been leading—right into Ah-ji's bed, that's what. Everybody knows you're not satisfied if you don't run off to him every couple of days to get laid!"

"You shut up! If I hear any more of that filth, I'll . . ." Auntie Ah-wang was shouting with such ferocity that her face was all twisted.

On the other hand, her daughter-in-law, secure inside the house, was just getting warmed up, and she kept up her verbal barrage: "Well, if you're not carrying on with Ah-ji, why did you give him the sacrificial chickens and ducks, when we don't even have enough for ourselves? Do you mean to tell me he doesn't have kids and grandkids of his own?"

Just when it seemed that nothing could stop Harmony, her mother-in-law, who was shaking like a leaf by then, plopped down on the ground, her lips ashen and trembling, unable to make a single sound. Her normally smooth and shiny bun had come undone, scattering her gray hair all about her face as she sat there staring straight ahead.

Some neighbor women rushed over to briskly rub her back and massage her chest. They were all talking a mile a minute. Just then, Auntie Ah-wang's son pushed his way through the crowd of onlookers. He was a robust man of medium build. Putting down his carrying pole and baskets, which were half-filled with fish, he strode over to the house, knocked twice on the door, and said in a level tone:

"Harmony, it's me. Open the door."

When she heard her husband's voice—she had stopped yelling when the commotion died down outside—she went to the door without a second thought. But no sooner had she opened the door and greeted her husband—"Ah-qing!"—than he burst into the house, grabbed her by the hair, and dragged her outside. With a resounding slap across each cheek, he sent her reeling. She fell to the ground, blood trickling from the corner of her mouth. Then he started kicking her for all he was worth. She tried to protect her abdomen with her arms and by rolling her body up into a ball. She was crying piteously. Still not satisfied, Ah-qing turned around, slipped the bamboo pole from the load he had left on the ground, and was raising it over his head to hit her when two or three fishermen in the crowd quickly restrained him.

"That's enough," they counseled him, "that's enough."

"You'll kill her if you don't watch out."

With an angry snort, he threw down the bamboo pole. Some more fishermen came up, forming a circle around him and, with their arms around his shoulders, hustled him off.

"Fuck 'em all. Come on over to my place and share a bottle of White Deer wine."

Once the men drifted away, the crowd of women also broke up, leaving behind only a couple of women about Harmony's age who worked the oyster beds with her. They helped her to her feet. Sobbing and moaning, she walked into the house, with an occasional cry of pain. She noisily opened chests and drawers, and made up a small bundle of clothing. She was going home to mother, she sobbed, vowing to never again set foot in this house as long as she lived. Finally she turned and walked out the door on the arms of her companions.

Auntie Ah-wang was still sitting silently on the ground. Several of the neighbor women tried to console her and offered to help her back into the house. Grandmother Gu, who enjoyed the distinction of being the oldest among them, pronounced judgment on the whole episode: "Your son avenged you by beating her, now don't you go and lower yourself to her level. Young people speak without using their heads. Don't pay any attention to her."

Auntie Ah-wang just kept staring straight ahead. Eventually she said: "Let me sit a while. I'll get up by myself when I'm up to it."

The same Wangshi who had washed clothes with her that morning thought that was a good idea: "She's right! I've heard that when old people fall down, you're supposed to let them get up on their own. Here, somebody bring a rattan stool over for her to lean on."

Someone was already bringing a stool over from the yard. She placed it under Auntie Ah-wang's arm.

Auntie Ah-wang boosted herself up, repeating: "Let me sit a while. I'll get up by myself." By then the women knew that she had cried and screamed herself out, and since it was getting late, they started heading home.

As the last ray of twilight faded away, darkness fell with a swiftness that one could almost feel. The whistling sea breezes grew more clamorous, swirling in from all directions, then lingering in that wide expanse between earth and sky, each gust a tragic howl.

Lin Shi had originally intended to go over and see how Auntie Ah-wang was doing, but Chen Jiangshui was already home. She knew he had always disliked this neighbor, and she wasn't about to do anything to anger him. She built a fire in the stove as fast as she could, then went outside on the pretext of drawing water from the large vat, making several trips altogether. Each time, she saw Auntie Ah-wang sitting there in the same position. The blue-white rays of the full moon, which had just climbed into the sky, shone down on Auntie Ah-wang's faded blue shirt, and for some reason, Lin Shi was reminded of the stiffly erect paper figures in the mourning tents waiting to be burned as offerings to the dead.

Not a sound came from Auntie Ah-wang—not even a sniffle—and Lin Shi could feel in her bones that something was not quite right. It wasn't as though Auntie Ah-wang had never quarreled with her daughter-in-law before. But in the past, the younger woman would always go flying tearfully home to her mother, and Auntie Ah-wang, with an admirable presence of mind, would sit by the door, weeping, sniffling, and lamenting: "How I suffer! Oh, how I suffer!" for all the world to hear. She would recount how she had reared her son at great personal sacrifice. Then, swearing to heaven and earth, she would wish a painful, lingering death on her daughter-in-law. It would go on like that for most of the evening.

But this time there wasn't a murmur, and Lin Shi found this puzzling. During dinner she couldn't stop herself from mentioning it to Chen Jiangshui, who merely uttered a muffled grunt to show his complete indifference.

After dinner, as Lin Shi was clearing the table, the sound of something heavy crashing to the floor came from next door. Assuming that the wind had knocked over something in the yard, she paid no notice. Chen Jiangshui, on the other hand, cocked his head and listened closely. Then, with a loud "Damn!" he picked up his butcher knife from the table and, kicking open the half-closed door, ran outside.

Lin Shi dropped what she was washing and followed him outside. He was already inside Auntie Ah-wang's house by the time Lin Shi was out the door. When Lin Shi arrived at her neighbor's house, she could see, by the faint light of the tiny electric bulb, Auntie Ah-wang stretched out on the ground, making choking and gurgling sounds. A rope about the thickness of two fingers was wrapped around her neck. With an upward flick of his wrist, Chen Jiangshui slashed it with his knife. The rope parted softly. Auntie Ah-wang's face had turned all puffy and purple. The air escaped from her in one big sigh.

Chen Jiangshui knelt on the ground beside Auntie Ah-wang and propped her up, massaging her chest to help her breathe.

"Get some water," he barked at Lin Shi, "and make it snappy!"

Lin Shi rummaged around frantically until she found a rice-bowl, which she filled to the brim with water. But her hands were trembling so much that nearly half of it had spilled by the time she reached them. Chen took the water from his wife and put it up to Auntie Ah-wang's lips. She sipped it slowly. When she had finished, Chen picked up her thin body with ease and laid her down on her bed. He turned and strode out the door without a backward glance, saying to Lin Shi: "You look after her. I'll go get Ah-qing."

Left alone in the house with her, Lin Shi experienced a nagging fear. Auntie Ah-wang lay on her side, facing the wall under the dim light of the single bulb, not so much as stirring. She had fixed the rope on a nail in the door frame beneath the lintel. Lin Shi spotted some pieces of broken wood that had fallen to the ground and now lay as mute testimony to what had almost happened. She was wondering why Auntie Ah-wang had attached the rope to the lintel, but then she looked up and realized that the mud house had no beams—that was the only place she could have tied it.

Backing away a little, Lin Shi crouched down beside the bed, trying unsuccessfully to dispel the vivid images that kept appearing before her eyes: Blood gushing from all seven apertures. Eyes turned up into the head. A protruding tongue more than a foot in length, all swollen and purple, lolling down on the chest.

She shook her head, telling herself: I saw her drinking water just a few minutes ago, so she *can't* be dead. Besides, Chen Jiangshui will be right back.

But Chen Jiangshui didn't come right back. Lin Shi became extremely sensitive to the passage of time. Outside the wind was still howling and whistling, growing louder with each gust. For a moment, she was convinced that Auntie Ah-wang was already dead, that she was keeping company with a corpse. Gripped by a terror that she had never before experienced, her stomach began to churn as though she were starving, nearly tying itself up into knots. The only rational thought she was capable of forming was of getting herself out of there as fast as her feet would carry her. But her legs were like rubber, and she just kept crouching there, unable to move. She hugged her legs with her arms as she shivered all over.

Eventually, Lin Shi heard herself calling out in a low, hoarse voice: "Auntie Ah-wang! Auntie Ah-wang!"

Even to her, it sounded as though she were summoning back the soul of the deceased, and she forced herself to stop. She held her breath for a moment, then called out again in a more controlled voice. But her calls hovered just below the low ceiling, pressing down on her with a crushing weight, like an inexhaustible force.

Lin Shi's calls grew more and more urgent, almost as though it might be too late if she didn't do something fast. After a while, Auntie Ah-wang groaned heavily and made choking sounds. This was followed by rapid, high-pitched, yet quiet, sobs. Every once in a while there was a pause in her sobs, which were replaced by heavy, labored breathing.

Lin Shi began to stir. With both hands on the floor, she tried to push herself to her feet, but her legs were so stiff and weak from crouching that she fell forward before she could catch herself.

Crawling over to Auntie Ah-wang's bed, she raised herself to a kneeling position by holding on to one of the legs. She reached out to stroke Auntie Ah-wang's shoulders. They were nothing but skin and bones, but at least they were warm. She sighed with relief and, inexplicably, burst into tears.

By the time Chen Jiangshui returned, Ah-qing in tow, Lin Shi had given herself over to sobbing. That was the sight that greeted Ah-qing as he entered the room. He ran up to the bed in panic, dropped down on both knees, and cried out with grief, "Mother!" before breaking down and weeping bitterly.

Chen Jiangshui, who was no less alarmed, also rushed over to the bed. Just then Auntie Ah-wang started to turn over in response to her son's voice. Chen Jiangshui struck Lin Shi with the back of his hand. "What the hell are you crying about? She's okay!"

Lin Shi was stunned. She stopped sobbing abruptly. Ah-qing, who was kneeling alongside her, turned and bowed deeply before her, saying slowly and clearly:

"You saved my mother's life. Let me kowtow three times to show my gratitude."

Lin Shi was too shocked to move. Ah-qing banged his head on the floor, producing a dull thud. After he straightened up, Lin Shi saw that his face was ruddy and puffy from drinking, but he was quite sober. His cloudy, bloodshot eyes had a look of calm devotion. Before Lin Shi could gather her wits, Ah-qing banged his head on the ground again. This so flustered her that she bent over until she was lying prostrate on the ground, from which position she heard the dull thud of the third kowtow, heavier and louder than the previous two. Stunned and alarmed, she dared not move and was uncertain of what to do next.

She felt Chen Jiangshui drag her to her feet. Before she knew it, she was back home. She didn't even have enough time to go over in her mind what had happened that evening, for Chen Jiangshui was already pressing her down on the bed and savagely tearing at her pants before finally collapsing on top of her.

Chen Jiangshui's desperate need terrified her. As if that weren't enough, the image of Auntie Ah-wang with a rope around her neck kept appearing before her eyes. With a strength summoned from some unknown source, she began to resist mightily. She bit. She scratched. She kicked with both feet. But that only fanned Chen Jiangshui's passion. Swearing obscenely, he warded off her attack as though it were all part of the game.

After nearly exhausting herself, she still hadn't been able to rid herself of the heavy body on top of her, and she finally stopped struggling. Just then an idea flashed into her mind.

"I'm having my you-know-what!" she exclaimed.

Chen Jiangshui froze. Panting heavily, he began to curse her. At first Lin Shi thought he was going to roll off her. Instead, he angrily reached down to feel her crotch and her pants. Slapping her so hard she saw stars, he really let fly with the curses: "Fuck your mother! You stinking whore, who do you think you're trying to fool? I'll fuck . . . fuck the life right out of you!"

Lin Shi was much too frightened to move, or to even make a sound. She just lay there enduring Chen Jiangshui's violent, rapid movements until she seemed on the verge of losing consciousness. Until all she could see were two eyes shining with a brutal light. Until her ears were filled with the sound of his labored breathing, mixed with a steady string of curses: "I'll fuck the life right out of you! I'll fuck the life right out of that stinking cunt of yours! I'll fuck the life . . . fuck the life right out of you!"

This went on and on and on. She felt she was coming apart. Finally it was over. No more curses. Chen Jiangshui had no sooner rolled off her than he was sound asleep and snoring loudly.

Lin Shi lay in the darkness. For a moment she was unable to

move, and it took a while before she was in control of her senses again. She thought about what Harmony had said about Auntie Ah-wang, how she had accused her of carrying on with Ah-ji. Was *this* what she was carrying on with Ah-ji for? Was *this* what she had almost hanged herself over? She wondered. If it was, then it was all beyond her ability to comprehend. She shook her head, feeling quite mystified. Hard though she tried, she could not come up with a satisfactory explanation. Meanwhile, outside, the sea winds grew more intense with each gust.

CHAPTER FIVE

Even before dawn had broken the next day, the news that Auntie Ah-wang had tried to hang herself was spreading among the early rising fishing folk in Chencuo. Lin Shi waited around for Auntie Ah-wang to come out and do the laundry with her. But when it became obvious that she wasn't going to show, Lin Shi gathered up the items that needed washing, her laundry basket, and the washboard, and went off to the well alone.

The dozen or so women at the well clammed up as soon as they caught sight of Lin Shi walking toward them. Wangshi made room for the latecomer by moving her pile of laundry aside.

"I hear that Pig-Butcher Chen saved Auntie Ah-wang's life," she greeted Lin Shi. "Were you there to help?"

Lin Shi was caught off guard, but she managed to nod in response.

"Did you actually see Auntie Ah-wang hanging there?" Spring Bough asked. She had been nursing a cold for several days, which made her sound a little hoarse, and still her voice was the shrillest around. Her question nearly brought the work at the well to a standstill. The women looked in Lin Shi's direction. Embarrassed, she lost her tongue altogether. Luckily, Grandmother Gu came to her rescue:

"She's probably still in shock from last night. Don't press her."

"She didn't actually hang herself!" Lin Shi blurted out. "The nail came loose and she crashed to the ground. Chen Jiangshui heard the noise and ran over and rescued her."

Disappointment showed on the faces of several of the women.

"Did her eyes bulge out? Was her tongue hanging out? Was blood oozing out all over?"

Lin Shi shook her head.

"Now, how could that be?" Spring Bough muttered.

"Oh, there was something!" Lin Shi suddenly recalled. "Her face was all puffy and purple, sort of like an eggplant."

Strange looks passed among the women, looks that mystified Lin Shi. She hoped she hadn't said anything wrong. This was the first time in her life she had ever spoken up in front of so many people, and her hands were shaking. You could have heard a pin drop as the women busily attended to their laundry. The silence was broken by Grandmother Gu, who cleared her throat before saying slowly: "Come on, you're all dying to say something, so just spit it out."

Glancing around to make sure there were no unwelcome guests, Wangshi spoke hesitantly, measuring her words: "Of course, this is only something I heard, not something I started. If I did, may lightning strike me dead . . ."

Naturally, her words fueled everyone's curiosity. There was a clamor for her to get on with her story.

"Well, I heard that Auntie Ah-wang didn't *really* want to hang herself, that it was all an act to scare people. Let's face it, who in her right mind would try to hang herself from a nail hammered into a door lintel? Isn't that just about the dumbest thing you've ever heard?" Once this was out, Wangshi hastened to add: "Now remember, I'm not the one who started that. I heard it from someone else."

This got an immediate response from a startled Lin Shi: "But she had a rope around her neck, and . . ."

"What do *you* know?" Spring Bough interrupted. "Do you know what kind of knot she used?"

Lin Shi shook her head.

"You see! How can you hang yourself with a fast knot?"

Lin Shi's jaw dropped. She was flabbergasted. Grandmother Gu, who was standing next to her, had to tug at her sleeve to get her attention.

"There's no point in rehashing all of this," she said solemnly. "You and Pig-Butcher Chen went over together to save Ah-wang. Now, a hanging ghost is the worst kind to tangle with, and since Ah-wang didn't die this time, her hanging ghost might just try to make things rough for you."

Her words were not lost on the women in the group, who waited breathlessly for her to continue.

"I doubt that Pig-Butcher Chen believes in this sort of thing, so when you get home, you're to ask Ah-qing to prepare a portion of pig's feet and noodles. Make sure the feet are tied up with red string. Then offer them up together with some ghost money. Oh, and set off a string of firecrackers, too. Is that clear?"

Lin Shi nodded woodenly, tears of fear streaming down her face.

Grandmother Gu patted her on the shoulder, turned to the others, and said: "It was sheer luck that she survived at all. But here the rest of you are standing around saying bad things about her. Aren't you afraid . . ."

"I told you, I heard it from someone else. It wasn't me who started all this talk," Wangshi hastened to defend herself.

"Me, too," Spring Bough added. "Auntie Ah-wang's not the type to *really* kill herself."

"What if she were?" Grandmother Gu asked with growing anger. "If you were going to kill yourself, how much thought would you give to whether it was a slip knot or a fast knot?"

Spring Bough turned her head and spat noisily, muttering under her breath but not answering the question.

Lin Shi kept her head lowered as she quickly washed the few items she had brought, wrung them dry, and put them into her laundry basket. As she rose to leave, Grandmother Gu took hold of her hand.

"Do you remember what I told you?"

Lin Shi nodded, her eyes reddening.

As she walked off, Lin Shi recalled Chrysanthemum, who had thrown herself down the well and had come back as a ghost. If I decided to end it all someday, she thought, I'd jump down a well instead of scaring everybody like Auntie Ah-wang did. I sure wouldn't let everybody laugh at me over a fast knot or slip knot.

Head bowed, she walked home slowly, worrying about how to broach the subject of pig's feet and noodles with Chen Jiangshui and Ah-qing. As she walked into the house, she raised her head to see a houseful of people, silently sitting or standing. In the middle of the room sat Uncle Laifa, the current elder of Chencuo. To her surprise, even Ah-qing was there. Her heart was gripped by a momentary anxiety. Quickly lowering her head, she walked into the bedroom.

Since there was only a curtain between the living room and

bedroom, Lin Shi put her laundry basket down on the floor, then crouched in a corner and listened attentively. The silence caused by her arrival was broken by the dignified yet quavering voice of Uncle Laifa: "There's nothing to worry about. I don't think we need a send-off for the hanging ghost. That would just frighten all the neighbors. Spirits always come visiting at night after Dead Souls' Festival, anyway. Just be on the lookout, that's all."

This was followed by a fit of dry coughing and spitting.

"I'll take care of everything for you," the same voice continued. "Chen Jiangshui, Chen Ah-qing, is that all right with both of you?"

Lin Shi heard Chen Jiangshui answer in the affirmative and Ah-qing reply, "Just as you say." This was followed immediately by the sound of objects being moved and shifted about. Soon the house was filled with the scent of joss sticks and the pungent odor of burning paper. Smoke was everywhere. Finally, the air was rent by the earth-shaking noise of exploding firecrackers.

Lin Shi waited until everything was quiet before emerging from the bedroom. She was greeted by the sight of a large bamboo tray, which had been placed on the Eight-Immortals table. On top of it were two blackened pig's feet, wrapped together with strips of red paper an inch or so in width. The cooked pig's feet reeked of grease and were coated with an oily sheen. Several packets of noodles lay off to the side, still wrapped in the original red string from the shop where they had been purchased.

The smoke curling up from the joss sticks continued to emit a heady fragrance that filled the poorly lit mud house. It was nearly noon. The ends of the joss sticks glowed softly but persistently, giving off a reddish light that faintly illuminated the portrait of Laozi hanging on the wall, lending it a mysterious, faraway look.

The thick, meaty pig's feet, the several packets of fine noodles, the heavy aroma of incense, the shreds of paper from the firecrackers that covered the floor, all helped to settle Lin Shi's nerves. Standing in front of the table, she placed her palms together reverently, closed her eyes, and prayed softly, her heart filled with devotion: "Goddess Mazu, Goddess of Mercy Guanyin, please protect Ah-jiang and me. Ah-jiang's real name is Chen Jiangshui. He's a pig-butcher. I'm his wife. My name is Lin Shi. We disturbed a hanging ghost, but it all happened because we saved the life of Auntie Ah-wang, our neighbor. She couldn't see her way out of some trouble and tried to hang herself. Ah-jiang and I didn't mean anything bad by saving her. Goddess Mazu, you have to protect Ah-jiang and me. Don't let us be taken away by the hanging ghost."

This act of devotion reassured her. Seeing that it was nearly lunchtime, she started a fire in the stove and washed the rice. But her mind kept going back to those thick, meaty pig's feet. Several times she went into the other room to take a peek at them, but something kept holding her back whenever she was tempted to take them from the table.

According to local custom, once the ghost money had been burned, one could safely assume that the spirits had already feasted and the sacrifices could then be enjoyed by mortals. It so happened that there wasn't much food in the house that day, and Lin Shi was dying to taste the pig's feet and noodles, something she had never tried before. All she had to do was walk over to the table and pick it up. But she could not do it. The longer the sacrificial food is out there, she assured herself, the better the chances that the spirit will protect us. When Ah-jiang comes home, I'll ask him to take it off the altar so we can eat it for dinner.

She was concentrating so hard on the food in the other room that she forgot about the meal she was cooking in this one; as a result, she missed the moment when she should have mixed the sweet-potato mash into the rice, and by the time she remembered, the rice was already cooked and the water completely evaporated. It was too late to add the mash now. Her only thought was that Chen Jiangshui would be angry with her.

Sure enough, when he saw nothing but rice in his bowl, he slapped her across the face.

"You're determined to eat me out of house and home, aren't you? Don't forget, it wasn't all that long ago when you didn't even have sweet-potato mash to eat!"

Lin Shi lowered her head and kept quiet.

Chen Jiangshui shoveled some rice into his mouth. Looking down at the table, where there was only some spinach and some dried fish, he growled:

"Why is that all we've got? Did you finish off everything else?"

"You haven't brought anything back for several days," Lin Shi answered plaintively. She glanced over at the table-altar, then blurted out: "Why don't I slice up some of those pig's feet?"

Chen Jiangshui stopped eating, as though the idea had never occurred to him. But he didn't say a word. Nor did he even glance in the direction of the pig's feet. In what seemed like only three or four mouthfuls, he finished off the spinach and dried fish with a couple of bowls of rice, slammed down his chopsticks and bowl, and stormed out the door.

That afternoon Lin Shi sat in the doorway waiting for Auntie Ah-wang to come over and sit for a while, as she had always done before, so she could get some advice on how to handle the matter of the pig's feet. She waited and waited, but Auntie Ah-wang never came. Before Lin Shi knew it, she had begun to doze off as she leaned against the door. Lulled by an occasional sea breeze, she soon fell fast asleep.

Her dreams that summer afternoon were disturbing and confusing: She went over, took down the pig's feet, and cooked them with the noodles. But when she picked them up with her chopsticks, every one of those long, skinny noodles turned into a protruding purple tongue. Dark red blood oozed from the cuts she made in the pig's feet, but she kept stuffing the meat and noodles into her mouth until her eyes bulged and her throat was squeezed tighter and tighter.

At that moment she woke up with a start. Though she massaged it for a long time, her neck remained stiff and sore from having fallen asleep in a chair in that position.

Chen Jiangshui returned home later than usual that night. His face darkened the minute he walked in the door. He started drinking even before dinner was ready, ordering Lin Shi to give him some food to go with the wine. Steeling herself for the tongue-lashing or beating that would surely follow, she told him timidly that they didn't have anything for him to snack on. But to her astonishment, the slightly tipsy Chen Jiangshui said rather off-handedly: "Slice up some of those pig's feet."

A huge, dark fear crept into Lin Shi's heart.

"That was our offering to the hanging ghost," she said, overcome with anxiety.

"What do you mean, hanging ghost?" he asked, the sweep of his hand dismissing the very notion. "I'm not one of your yellow-bellied fishermen. I don't believe in evil spirits."

Lin Shi hesitated, not daring to move.

"Look at all those pigs I've killed. Nothing's happened to me yet, has it?" he said with a scornful laugh. "If your hanging ghost wants me, he can come and get me any time he pleases," he continued, as much to himself as to her.

Chen Jiangshui's willingness to bear the responsibility lessened Lin Shi's fears considerably. She took down the pig's feet, as he had told her to do, but when she sliced one of them open, she discovered that it had only been braised, leaving the meat inside all raw and bloody. She stared at the uncongealed blood. Dark and sticky, it reminded her of the purple blood oozing from the seven apertures in her dreams. That old, ominous fear returned.

After cooking the pig's feet in boiling water, Lin Shi ladled them, piece by piece, into a big bowl. Her stomach was churning up waves of nausea, and she had to turn her face away as she placed the unseasoned pig's feet on the table.

In no time, Chen Jiangshui, making sucking, slurping noises, was gnawing on one of the pig's feet. He found it puzzling that Lin Shi hadn't even picked up her chopsticks.

"Aren't you the one who loves to sneak food," he mocked her. "The chicken with the crooked beak finally gets to eat some nice rice, but winds up letting it go to waste instead. Where's all this phony politeness going to get you? Come on, dig in."

Not saying a word, Lin Shi ignored him. He tried several other tacks, but nothing worked. Starting to get angry, he smacked the table hard with his hand, causing the bowls and dishes to rattle loudly.

"You start eating or I'll beat the hell out of you!" he threatened savagely.

Lin Shi obediently picked up a piece and put it into her mouth. Nothing special. Another bite, and this time her mouth seemed to be filled with a gooey, gelatinous mess. Not only did the pig's feet taste worse than she had imagined they would, but the skin, tendons, and fat made them as tough and chewy as a piece of old dried fish skin. She swallowed the next mouthful after barely chewing it at all.

Chen Jiangshui got such a big kick out of watching the face she made every time she swallowed a mouthful that he roared with laughter and kept filling her bowl with more. She could barely get it down. Fortunately there was more bone than meat, and eventually it was all gone.

But Chen Jiangshui, who didn't want the show to end so soon, got to his feet and staggered into the kitchen, where he tore off a big chunk of the pig's leg. He tossed it down in front of Lin Shi.

"Eat, eat, eat!" he commanded her. "No one can accuse me of being stingy. Not after I let my wife eat an entire pig's leg."

The section where the foot was connected to the leg had only been partially cooked, and the layers of flesh beneath the skin were still nearly raw. Bright red blood seeped out from the center, giving off a rank odor. Lin Shi took one look at the big hunk of bloody meat in her hands and noisily threw up everything she had eaten. When her stomach was nearly empty, she had the dry heaves, then vomited yellow bile.

All this retching left her drained yet agitated. That night she tossed and turned as she was visited by strange, disjointed dreams. She awoke with a start, and the dreams were gone. She vaguely heard a cock crow and, seeing it was still pitch-dark outside, went back to sleep.

But not for long. Someone was taking off her pants. She was too sleepy; she didn't want to wake up.

"I'm having my you-know-what," she mumbled.

Smack! Smack! He slapped her twice. Her eyes snapped open, as Chen Jiangshui mocked her: "Trying to fool me with that again, hm? Well, it's not going to work."

"This time it's true," Lin Shi argued weakly.

Chen Jiangshui laughed derisively in the darkness, then took her. He didn't pinch or hit her this time, nor was he especially brutal. But it lasted a very long time. Lin Shi lay there on her back. This was the first time she had been assaulted during her period, and the idea so frightened her that she thought she was going to die for sure. In her anguish she could only weep and moan. The murky gloom outside sluggishly gave way to dawn. As Chen Jiangshui rolled off her, he could see by the first rays of the morning light that the lower part of his body was covered with dirty, dark red blood. The bed and the woman's lower parts were also smeared with dirty, rust-colored clots of blood.

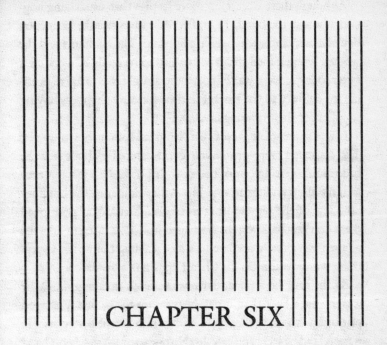

CHAPTER SIX

Because the month-long observance of the Dead Souls' Festival is staggered by district, the seventh month isn't a particularly busy time for pig-butchers, at least not when compared to New Year's or the Emperor of Heaven's birthday. Of course, the people in some of the districts—places like Jinsheng Lane, which observes the thirteenth, or Xinghua Mazu Palace, which observes the ninth—spend a great deal of money on offerings during the festival, since they are located in the heart of Lucheng. The inhabitants of these "uptown" districts are shopowners who also rent out farmland in the outlying areas, so their standard of living is beyond the reach of the fishing folk of Chencuo or the farmers. Naturally the "uptown" butchers are kept pretty busy.

Although there were a few more fat pigs than usual lying hog-tied awaiting the butcher's knife on the seventeenth, Chencuo's day of observance, they weren't lined up. The assistants and the women who cleaned the carcasses had to be ready to work a bit faster today, since it was important to slaughter as many as possible for delivery to the market in time for early shoppers buying supplies for their offerings.

It was getting late, and Chen Jiangshui hadn't shown up yet. The assistants were grumbling good-naturedly about how he had trouble getting out of bed now that he had a wife. But they weren't just standing around idly—they tightened the bindings on a few of the pigs waiting to be slaughtered and positioned them on their backs on the V-shaped platforms. Meanwhile, the women had already prepared a vat of scalding hot water. Everything was in readiness for Chen Jiangshui's arrival.

By the time he arrived, dawn was already breaking. Since he was so much later than usual, he went up to the first V-shaped platform without bothering to change into his rubber boots. He was greeted by jeers and catcalls. No one so much as saw his hand move, but a full-grown pig weighing four or five hundred catties let out a long, pitiful squeal and was wracked by convulsions.

As soon as Chen Jiangshui's hand moved away, the pig's head slumped sideways and a geyser of blood shot forth in a column some seven or eight inches high. There was a great deal of blood, all foamy and frothy. Though women were standing by with containers to catch the blood, some of it spilled, especially during the animal's death throes, when it splattered the platform itself.

After a minute or two, when the animal had been pretty well bled and its struggles and squeals had grown feeble, the assistants hauled it off the platform and dumped it onto the floor. The pig continued to twitch at intervals, its blood still spurting from the gash in its throat, staining the floor around it and filling the air with its stench.

This was Chen Jiangshui's moment. As the knife was withdrawn and the blood spurted forth, he was infused with an incomparable sense of satisfaction. It was as though the hot stream coursing through his body was converted into a thick, sticky white fluid spurting into the shadowy depths of a woman at the climax of a series of high-speed thrusts. To Chen Jiangshui, the spurting of blood and the ejaculation of semen had the same orgasmic effect.

But on that particular morning, the day of Chencuo's festival observation, the sight of that splattered red blood reminded Chen Jiangshui of the rust-colored splotches of menstrual blood on the bed that morning. An unnamed fury and a chilling fear caused him to shiver with apprehension.

He couldn't just ignore the popular belief that contact with menstrual blood brought bad luck to a man, especially considering the bloody nature of his occupation. Good omens were more important than anything else. Chen Jiangshui cursed himself inwardly. He couldn't forgive himself for being so careless. "Stupid!" he mumbled. "Fuck! How stupid can you be! Fuck!"

Work in the slaughterhouse advanced like wildfire. As each pig was dumped onto the floor, the women rushed up and dragged the bled animal over to the well, where they scooped out water and washed the carcass from head to tail. Then they rolled it into a trough filled with boiling water and stripped the hide of its bristles. The water was boiled at the far end of the killing floor, opposite the well. A wood-fueled fire was kept going in a brick fireplace under a huge cauldron of water. When the water came to a boil, it was poured into the trough and the cauldron was refilled with cold water.

Meanwhile, even though an unnamed fury filled Chen Jiangshui's heart, an instinct bred of years of experience carried him to the next platform, knife in hand. Another team of assistants had a second pig firmly pressed against the V-shaped surface, waiting for Chen Jiangshui. The process was repeated.

Again and again it repeated itself, as Chen Jiangshui steadied the knife in his hand, gradually losing himself in his work. Then, discovering that he had spilled the blood of nearly a dozen pigs, he stopped abruptly. Looking behind him, he saw that the first pig had already had its bristles removed and was washed clean; it was hanging upside down, its hind legs chained to a metal ring above one of the platforms, waiting for him to come over and slice open its abdomen.

Usually at this point Chen Jiangshui would crack a few dirty jokes with the assistants as he approached the animal. Leisurely raising the knife in his hand, he would then sink it into the pig's chest, and with one downward slice, the pig's abdomen would burst open with a pop. No blood, just a bellyful of grayish viscera hanging there. As if on signal, the assistants would come forward to retrieve the edible organs from the mess and take down the suspended carcass. Even then there would be a trace of dark red blood trickling out of the pig's mouth and slit throat.

It was a different scene on this particular morning. Since Chen Jiangshui had arrived late, there was no bantering about women. Though he appeared to be concentrating more than usual on the business of slitting open the pigs' abdomens, he failed to plunge the knife in deeply enough, so that he didn't cut all the way through the flesh. A second cut was needed, leaving a ragged opening. This happened very rarely, and when it did, Chen would spit loudly on the floor and direct savage curses at whatever it was that had triggered his bad luck. On this festival morning he missed repeatedly, sometimes cutting so deeply he damaged the intestines and other internal organs, and sometimes not cutting deeply enough. Yet, not a sound from Chen Jiangshui.

"Must have been working too hard last night!" mocked one of the assistants, who knew how to wield a knife. "Want me to take over?"

Chen Jiangshui shook his head, but said nothing. He was the picture of seriousness as he mustered all his strength to control the butcher knife he was holding, gripping it so tightly his hand began to tremble.

After missing several times, Chen Jiangshui could feel that his hands were gradually steadying. He took a deep breath and released it slowly. Sensing the energy coursing unimpeded from his shoulder all the way down to his wrist, he raised his arm and struck. With a single pass of the razor-sharp blade, the pig's abdomen opened softly, as though it had been unzipped, from the throat straight down. Perfect.

Chen Jiangshui stood still. He grinned broadly and spat loudly on the floor. The morning scene of rust-colored menstrual blood all over the bed flashed through his mind. He frowned and spat noisily several times.

The wrap-up work went like clockwork. The disemboweled pigs were moved into a small room and hung upside down by their hind legs from iron rings. Then the people responsible for branding came up with their rollers and stamped row after row of purplish brands on the skin, not forgetting, of course, the tops of the pigs' heads. When they were finished, the assistants came forward and severed each animal's head at the base of the neck.

The disemboweled pigs were then laid out, together with the heads and viscera, on the floorboards of rickshaws pulled by the meat vendors. Whether the pork would be sold together with the skin and bones or in choice chunks of lean meat depended on the skill of the meatcutter who sold it to the customers.

On this festival morning, everyone was in such a rush to get the meat to market that Chen Jiangshui went into the small room to help cut the heads off. As he was severing the head of a large, meaty pig, he turned and asked the short, middle-aged man stand-ing beside him: "Hey, Ah-bian. This pig of yours . . . promised to anyone?"

The man called Ah-bian shook his head.

"Then let me have the head."

"Sure. You can have it at the regular price." Ah-bian slapped him on the shoulder. "You understand that it's festival time, and pig's head is one of the three sacrificial offerings—I could get a pretty good price for this."

After threading a rope through the snout and binding the head securely, Chen Jiangshui carried it out of the slaughterhouse by the other end of the rope. The sun had already climbed high in the sky. It was another one of those sunny midsummer days without a cloud in the sky for miles. The sun's shimmering rays poured down, shining directly on the soft pale gold of the neigh-boring wheatfield, which was turning yellow from the forming ears of grain. The light breeze that blew in from the surrounding empty countryside was soft and carried a hint of warmth.

It was going to be one of those hot, muggy days. Chen Jiang-shui walked down the narrow path, the tall bamboo on both sides rustling in the wind. He stopped and leaned against a thick stalk of bamboo, trying to decide where he wanted to go. At this hour, short of going home to face Lin Shi with her long face and the frightened look that always adorned it, where could he go? He thought hard, his frustration mounting. Just then an idea crept into his head—Golden Flower, of course. That snug bed of Golden Flower's, all warmed from sleep, was just what he needed.

A narrow path that meandered through ricefields led from the slaughterhouse to Backstreet. A ten-minute walk at most. The place called Backstreet was the area behind one of Lucheng's big streets; it consisted of a lane with a row of ten or so buildings on each side. They were all single-story frame buildings except for one that was two stories tall and dated from the Qing dynasty. It was named the House of Moonlight Pleasures. In the past, a row of high-backed chairs would have been arranged in a semicircle on the second-story balcony, known as the Balustrade of Beauties. In the evening, these chairs would have been filled with prostitutes casting enticing glances toward the would-be clients passing below. It had been the talk of the town in Lucheng. In those days, of course, the women were said to be skilled poets, painters, and musicians—entertaining with their artistic talents, selling their smiles but not their bodies—and were called artistes.

Many years had passed since those days, and the Balustrade of Beauties had suffered from long neglect. All that remained were a few loose, rotting boards. No one dared go near it. The Balustrade of Beauties existed in legend only, for no "artistes" were in residence at the House of Moonlight Pleasures. Refined scholars and wealthy merchants no longer congregated there, and the building itself was in a very sorry state. A plaque inscribed with the words "Of Matters Pertaining to Moonlight Pleasures" (said to have been the gift of an eminent scholar) hung lopsided above the entrance. The words, written in a florid style and etched with gold, had also suffered from the ravages of time and the elements, and they no longer seemed to float in the air.

But none of this altered the fact that the House of Moonlight Pleasures still boasted the more "respectable" of the Backstreet women. What this meant, of course, was that they were generally younger and better looking than the others. Nevertheless, they were a far cry from their Qing dynasty predecessors—they had no skills as poets or painters, nor could they get by with selling only their smiles and not their bodies. And so, like all the other Backstreet women, they were referred to by the Lucheng townspeople as "professional women."

All those tales of refined scholars and elegant gentlemen amusing themselves with courtesans meant nothing to Chen Jiangshui. That the House of Moonlight Pleasures had such a genteel past was nothing compared to having a woman pinned beneath him, her legs spread wide. If he could ask for anything else, it would be that she would scream her head off the whole time. And as far as he was concerned, the young women at the House of Moonlight Pleasures had no talent at this.

So he had chosen Springtime House and the warm bed of Golden Flower. In spite of the repeated mocking of his fellow butchers that he needed to suckle at a mother's breast again, Chen Jiangshui had come for Golden Flower almost exclusively all these years. Eventually, the other women in Backstreet came to understand that what Chen Jiangshui was so fond of were Golden Flower's sexy screams.

On this festival morning, Chen Jiangshui entered Backstreet, walking along the stone-paved road that was the only reminder of the area's former splendor. The entire surface was paved with gray granite blocks, each of them some three or four feet long and a foot wide, arranged in a simple crisscross pattern. Since this road never turned into a muddy quagmire, clients could be seen coming and going at all times.

When Chen Jiangshui arrived at Springtime House, the two aging wooden doors were tightly shut, as always. It had been a while since his last visit, and everything seemed somehow unfamiliar. He couldn't say just why. He wondered how much turnover there had been among the women during that period and whether the old madam was still around. Well, he'd know soon enough.

If Golden Flower was still there, hers would be the room on the right, over there, facing the street. He knocked loudly on the wooden bars covering the window.

"Golden Flower!" he shouted. "Golden Flower, open up! It's me!"

Whenever Golden Flower had a client who had spent the night, the old madam would come to the door. "You're pretty early," she would chide him good-naturedly as she opened the door. "You'll wake everybody up." But if Golden Flower was alone, she would get out of bed and lazily drape a shirt over her shoulders. Without even bothering to button up, she would hold the front closed at the collar with one hand and unbolt the door with the other, peering through the crack of the partially opened door to see who it was.

In his impatience for someone to open up, Chen Jiangshui was about to knock again when the door creaked open. He walked in. The bright summer rays of July filtered in just enough to faintly illuminate the room. He saw the figure of a woman with a shirt draped loosely around her shoulders. Since she had to use both hands to open the door, her full, pendulous breasts were exposed. Although it was very dark, he recognized her at once.

"Golden Flower, it's me."

There was a note of urgency in Chen Jiangshui's voice. No sooner was he all the way inside the room than he reached out to fondle and squeeze her full, drooping breasts. She just stood there, neither welcoming nor shrinking from his attentions until he let his hands drop. She led him into her room.

It was small and narrow, about six or seven feet wide. She reached up and twisted a tiny light bulb in its socket. The dim light revealed a wooden bed and a bamboo chair off to one side. A white bedsheet with a red embroidered design at the top covered the bed, although the white part was covered with dark stains and was so soiled it was more gray than white. The woman climbed up onto the bed, removed the shirt she had draped over her shoulders, and lay down on her back, pulling the bedsheet up to cover her belly. "Everyone wants to stay cool in the summer, but they're afraid of catching cold if they fall asleep." She had a rough-sounding voice, her accent identifying her as someone from the countryside, with that telltale rise on ending syllables.

Fastening the rope to a nail in the wall, Chen Jiangshui carefully hung the pig's head up. Then he shed his clothes and heaved his heavy, hairy body up onto the bed next to Golden Flower. He also dragged a corner of the bedsheet up to cover the lower half of his body. The woman waited until he was settled before continuing:

"You haven't been by for a long time." She paused, then continued matter-of-factly: "In fact, you stopped coming as soon as you got married."

Chen Jiangshui didn't respond. He turned her over on her side and buried his face between her full breasts, inhaling deeply. Having been roused from her sleep, she still smelled warm and sweet—a fragrance of body and of bed, a warmth reminiscent of the night. Chen Jiangshui buried his face between her breasts, seeking a space that felt comfortable. "I'm going to doze for a while first," he said before falling asleep.

The woman lay tranquilly on her side, her eyes open. She had a flat, broad face with large eyes and thick, open lips. At first glance she appeared somewhat dull-witted, although not without a certain lethargic sweetness—the latter probably due to her profession. She had the strong body of a peasant woman who was used to hard work, and a pair of large, work-hardened hands. In recent years, owing to a lack of physical activity and to the aging process in general, her body had grown slack and heavy. Yet there were still traces in her plumpness of a healthy vigor born of past labor. She had, as a result, a quality of ease about her. Her skin still retained its copper tan and her body resembled nothing so much as a water-soaked field after autumn harvest.

She lay there with her eyes open, watching Chen Jiangshui sleep. He wasn't going to be waking up soon. It was a quiet, peaceful morning in Backstreet, so quiet that she could hear the vendors out on the street. The room was warm, the air stale and heavy. She closed her eyes, and before long she, too, fell asleep, snoring softly.

How much later she didn't know, she felt Chen Jiangshui stirring at her breasts. Though still not quite awake, she instinctively assumed that he wanted her, so she rolled onto her back and assumed the position. But rather than make a move toward her, he said cheerfully:

"I slept like a baby. That makes up for all the poor sleep I've had lately."

Her eyes remained closed, and she said nothing, keeping her legs open and raised a while longer, just in case. But still he failed to mount her.

"Don't you want it?" she finally asked him.

"I screwed my old lady this morning and got her blood all over me," he answered dejectedly.

She giggled.

"You're quite the eager beaver, aren't you? Well, I can't really blame you. According to what I've heard from people around Chencuo, that wife of yours is really something. She loves it so much that people three miles away can hear her screams."

"She could still take lessons from you." Chen Jiangshui, who was starting to get into the mood, moved his face up closer to hers.

"It's all a put-on anyway," she said candidly with an open laugh, revealing two rows of strong white teeth. "You've been away so long I'm out of practice. I probably couldn't scream if I wanted to."

"You crazy broad," Chen Jiangshui said softly, tenderly.

The two of them lay without speaking for a while. Then she said casually: "I'm going to quit soon."

"Hm?"

"My mother-in-law wants me to come back. She said she'll let me adopt my brother-in-law's youngest son."

"And you agreed?" The excitable Chen Jiangshui pushed himself up into a sitting position. "All they really want is your money."

"I know." There wasn't a hint of surprise in her voice. "But if I keep on like this, it'll never end. I'll wind up being a madam when I'm forty or fifty, then I'll have to force other women to work to keep food on my table . . ."

Her voice trailed off, and Chen Jiangshui kept silent. Finally, he asked her abruptly: "Are you still willing to go back there after the way they drove you out when your husband died?"

"That was because I didn't have any children." She reached down and stroked her belly compassionately. "I don't know why this belly of mine can't even produce a cockroach."

"Golden Flower," Chen Jiangshui said anxiously. "If you go back you'll have to work the fields. Think you can stand it?"

The woman wiggled her toes. She had large feet with splayed toes, the kind that spend the entire year stomping around in mud.

"I've been dreaming a lot lately. It's always the same dream—the sow back home has a litter of twenty-five little pigs, but since she doesn't have any milk, the little ones all run up to me.

"I went over to the Dragon Hill Temple to seek advice from the Guanyin Bodhisattva. The abbot there explained the meaning of the dream to me. He said that since my mother-in-law has been having bad harvests these past few winters, she's coming to me for food, just like the little pigs."

She was rambling on, but when she got to this point she recalled Chen Jiangshui's question.

"Even if the work is hard, it'll be better than my life here."

"Maybe it's a good idea, after all. At least it'll bring an end to this." He thought for a moment, then went on: "But hold on to your money, and don't forget how they drove you out."

"Don't worry." She smiled a bright, detached smile.

"So when are you going back?"

"My mother-in-law was here a couple of days ago to get some money. She wanted me to go back with her then, but I figured I ought to work a little longer. A regiment of soldiers was transferred over this way a while ago, and business has been booming."

"I'll never hear your screams again." Chen Jiangshui patted her plump, round bottom. "I'll never be able to screw you again."

"You can always come look me up in my village."

"You crazy broad," Chen Jiangshui chided her.

They looked at each other and laughed.

The two of them lay in bed together, Chen Jiangshui listening to the woman as she told how her mother-in-law had borrowed money from her to buy a sow. They were expecting it to give birth any day now. Once the pigs were born and raised to adulthood, the family would have a little money of its own. A small amount had already been set aside to buy back a little land, and with some pigs and enough land, they wouldn't have to worry about going hungry. All this talk about pigs reminded the woman of something, and she turned to Chen.

"Later," she said, "whenever I need a pig butchered, I'll ask you to come help me out."

Chen Jiangshui laughed loudly.

"Aren't you afraid you'll get arrested for killing a pig on the sly?"

"How can it be 'on the sly' if it's my own pig?" she said indignantly.

"You crazy broad, don't you know anything?"

Chen Jiangshui spoke to her in a lecturing tone of voice. He patiently explained how you had to have an official brand on every pig that was butchered, how you had to pay taxes, and things like that. Knowing that he was just showing off how much he knew about his specialty, she didn't pay much attention. Her large, yet somewhat dimmed and swollen eyes stared straight ahead at nothing in particular. For the sake of conversation, she casually commented, "Oh, I see!" from time to time during Chen's explanation.

But as soon as Chen Jiangshui had said his piece, she countered deftly:

"I'd only be butchering my own pig for food. And whatever we couldn't eat ourselves, we'd share with relatives in the village. Do you mean to say they'd expect me to pay a tax on top of that? What kind of justice is that?"

"That's the fucking way it is!" Chen Jiangshui held her around the waist. "Fortunately, they don't deduct the stamp fee from my pay. If they tried that, I sure wouldn't fucking let them get away with it." He was getting angry without knowing just why. A surge of fury began to fill his head. His temples throbbed violently, his sunken eyes flashed.

"Golden Flower, now you listen to me. If anyone ever tries anything with you, you come look me up at the slaughterhouse. I'll settle the score with my butcher knife."

"I will," she said tenderly, calmly, resting her cheek against his. "I don't want you to be like this. It's like you're about to slaughter a pig."

"I know. I get like this whenever I'm upset."

Chen Jiangshui said this helplessly, weakly. The excitement that he had felt just a moment before, the intensely focused energy that made him feel like he was about to attack, had all dissipated. It was replaced by a depressing, vast sense of emptiness.

"It's not only that you have to pay a tax to butcher a pig—there are even people who have jurisdiction over pig droppings!"

The woman gave a perfunctory grunt.

"I was out collecting pig manure by the time I was five years old. My manure basket was almost as tall as I was. It made my mom so sad that she'd put her arms around me and cry. She had to make bean curd for a living."

"No kidding!" It was obvious that she had heard stories like this many, many times before, and there was no longer any real sympathy in her heart, but still she listened quietly and attentively.

"One time I was lucky and found a whole lot of manure. I never figured it might be too much for me to manage, so I just filled the basket up. But when I tossed it over my shoulder I fell over from the weight. Since I wasn't about to leave it for someone else, I started dragging it behind me. But before I was halfway home a couple of kids beat me up and ran off with my basket."

"Mm," the woman said softly.

"My mom had to go out to make bean curd in the middle of the night, but before she left, she spent all evening weaving me another basket. I wasn't more than seven or eight then, but I swore I'd get even one day."

"And did you?" she asked with a giggle. Even knowing the outcome of the story wasn't enough to stay her interest.

"I sure as hell did. After I started working at the slaughterhouse and made a few friends, I waylaid the two of them on the road one day and beat the hell out of them. Old Ah-gan's son was laid up in bed for several days. Ah-chun's son got off a little easier, but he damn near lost an eye."

"You shouldn't be like that," the woman said solemnly. "You know the Guanyin Bodhisattva says that kindness will be rewarded and evil will be punished . . . ."

"That's right," Chen Jiangshui interrupted her. "Being beaten up by me was their punishment."

She chuckled.

"You always have to have the last word, don't you? But I've heard people say that no matter what, you've got to leave yourself a way out for the future."

Chen Jiangshui nodded in agreement.

"My favorite story is about the time you used to peddle peanuts." She gave his heavy shoulder a nudge. "Tell it to me."

Chen Jiangshui grew a little bashful, but he went ahead anyway.

"Well, I used to peddle peanuts when I was a kid. My mother would cook them in their shells and put them in a basket for me to go out and peddle. It rained a lot one year for some reason, and I sold a whole lot of peanuts. Reason was . . ."

"Reason was," she cut in, "since the kids couldn't play outside, they ran wild indoors, and the adults bought them peanuts to keep them busy."

Chen Jiangshui laughed darkly.

"Since you know it so well, why don't you tell it?"

"I like to hear you tell it." She gazed off into a corner of the room. "Whenever the soldiers come, they tell me lots of strange things."

"Like what?"

"Like how they amuse themselves with other people's wives." She resumed her nonchalance. "You still haven't told that part about when the water came all the way up to your chest."

Chen Jiangshui continued compliantly: "Well, one time it rained so hard everything got flooded. At first the water in the Temple of the City God came up to my knees. I was afraid the peanuts in my basket would get all moldy if I didn't hurry up and sell them. But the water kept rising and rising, and before I knew it, it was up to my chest. It almost swept me away. Luckily there was a big banyan tree nearby, and I climbed up it as fast as I could."

"What happened to your basket and the peanuts?" she asked.

Chen Jiangshui laughed loudly. "How the hell should I know?"

"We farmers may not eat or dress all that well," she said as an afterthought, "but when I was small, we never went without at least a bowl of rice gruel mixed with sweet potatoes at home."

Chen Jiangshui's face clouded, and the conversation died. The two of them lay there listening to the intermittent cries of the street vendors outside, one in particular—an elderly man with a shrill voice—whose long, drawn-out cries of "SOFT—BEAN—CURD! ALMOND—TEA!" could be heard above all the others. The voice moved off down the road. By then there were sounds coming from some of the other rooms—people talking, doors opening, objects bumping and crashing. Chen Jiangshui yawned lazily, stretched, and got out of bed.

"I've got to go," he said.

The woman quickly got up and brought over his clothes from the bamboo chair. Taking them from her, Chen Jiangshui slipped into his local-made black wide-legged pants, then donned his short blue shirt, which had faded to a gray-blue after countless washings. He didn't bother to button up, leaving his greasy paunch exposed.

By that time the woman had already taken the pig's head down from the nail from which it had been hanging, and except for muttering, "Boy, that's heavy!" didn't say a word as she handed it over to Chen Jiangshui. Her equanimity and fatalistic presumption that the pig's head was not intended for her made Chen Jiangshui feel a little guilty.

"This is a sacrificial offering for the festival," he explained. "I'll bring some meat for you the next time I come."

The woman nodded, without saying a word, even when Chen Jiangshui took a wad of bills out of his pocket and handed them over to her. Since it was nearly noon, the room was getting stuffy. This time the woman didn't bother to drape the shirt over her shoulders, but just stood there naked and without any makeup on her face. With her feet apart and a slightly protruding belly, she really looked the part of a tired, heavy, thickset farming woman.

The dazzling white sunlight reflecting off the paving stones hurt Chen Jiangshui's eyes as he stepped out onto the street. "Fuck!" he muttered, squinting to keep the sun out of his eyes. Dangling the pig's head by the rope, and not really needing to look where he was going on this familiar path, he swaggered as he left Backstreet.

At home he was greeted by the sight of Lin Shi, her slight, skinny frame all huddled up on the bed. The gray cotton clothes she wore looked like a pile of rags. The only color was in her red, swollen cheeks, which on first glance could have been mistaken for a pair of plump, full chins. Not only did she look frightened, but she seemed to be in some sort of pain as well. The food had already been laid out on the table. Without even acknowledging her presence, Chen Jiangshui sat down and started to eat.

Looking up, he saw last night's leftover pig's feet lying on the table in front of him. He threw down his chopsticks and was about to curse, when he noticed that they had been cut into small pieces and stewed in soy sauce until they looked like a bowl of pork with the skin still on. They no longer bore any resemblance to the pig's feet that had been set out as a sacrificial offering. He picked up his chopsticks, hurriedly finished his meal, and walked swiftly out the door, leaving in his wake a single comment: "The pig's head is a sacrificial offering."

CHAPTER SEVEN

It is a Lucheng tradition that the Dead Souls' Festival is observed in the afternoon, starting around two or three o'clock and going straight through till sunset. With summer days being so long, that leaves a good four or five hours of sunlight for the observance. That much time is needed, the people believe, for the homeless ghosts released from the Temple of the City God to locate and eat the one good meal they can enjoy for the year.

Lin Shi had spent the morning of the festival at home feeling restless. Chen Jiangshui hadn't returned, and she still didn't know what she was going to use for an offering. On one of her many trips to the door to peer outside, she was rewarded by the sight of Ah-qing walking toward her with a fish at least two feet long in his arms.

He had caught it himself, he explained with a touch of shyness, and now he wanted to give it to them for use as an offering. It was nothing, really. He also took out a small cloth-wrapped bundle. From his wife, Harmony, he said, in appreciation to Lin Shi for saving her mother-in-law. He hastily handed the things over and rushed off, his face red with embarrassment.

Lin Shi didn't dare open the bundle, for fear that Chen Jiang-shui would give her hell if she did. Besides, it was getting late, time to go into the kitchen to clean and prepare the fish. She fried it to a golden brown and laid it out on a platter. It was so long that its tail hung over the side, so she quickly wedged a chopstick under the whole fish to support the tail. After having fretted the whole morning about not having an offering, the sight of this golden brown fish lying heavily on the platter went a long way toward putting Lin Shi at ease.

Her mood improved even more around noontime, when Chen Jiangshui came home carrying the large pig's head. Following the usual practice of preparing sacrificial animals, she boiled the head in a big pot of water, but since it was her first time, she didn't know exactly how long she should cook it. When she figured it was about done, she scooped it out and placed it in a closely woven bamboo sieve, since she couldn't find a platter large enough to hold it. The sight of the pig's head, which was nearly as large as the sieve, filled her heart with joy.

Lin Shi cooked a few vegetarian dishes, then hurried outside, where she set up a temporary altar next to the door using two rattan chairs and a long board. Seeing that her neighbors had long since finished their preparations and were already offering up prayers before lighted joss sticks, she hurriedly brought out the food she had prepared. The pig's head alone took up over half of the makeshift table; flanked by the big fish and the several vegetarian dishes, it was an offering she could be proud of.

After reverently lighting the joss sticks, she stood in the doorway facing out and carefully performed the rites over and over again. She exhorted the orphaned spirits and wandering ghosts to feast on the food she had prepared and begged the hanging ghost that had been spotted in the neighborhood recently to leave her and Ah-jiang alone.

When she had finished, she brought a rattan stool over and sat down by the door to protect her food against stray dogs and cats. She had no sooner gotten settled than she saw a group of five or six women coming in her direction. She jumped to her feet to get a better look. Walking at the head was none other than Auntie Ah-wang.

Auntie Ah-wang hadn't been to the well to do her laundry since the night she had been found lying unconscious on the floor, her face all red and puffy. Nor had she been about the neighborhood. So Lin Shi hadn't seen her in all this time, and for reasons she herself didn't understand, when she spotted Auntie Ah-wang walking up to her in the middle of that scorching afternoon, a cold shiver ran down her spine. Goosebumps covered her skin, and her scalp began to tingle.

Auntie Ah-wang was walking with the sun at her back, so that the golden afternoon rays of the midsummer sun spread a dazzling halo of light behind her. Set against that brilliant arc, she looked thinner and slighter than before, but she carried herself ramrod straight and held her head high. Though she walked with an unsteady gait, she was a very imposing figure.

As Auntie Ah-wang drew closer, Lin Shi noticed just how much weight she had lost. The white shirt that had turned gray from so many washings and her wide-legged black pants hung loosely on her. And her face had a wizened look. She had always had a sharp nose and a high forehead, but now her features stood out as clearly as if they had been etched.

Lin Shi called out impatiently before the older woman had even drawn up close to her: "Auntie Ah-wang! I haven't seen you in a long time!"

"Is that pig-butcher husband of yours at home?" Auntie Ah-wang asked flatly, cutting her off. Her head was still raised high.

"No, he's not. Auntie Ah-wang, I . . ."

Lin Shi was desperate to say something, but she'd never been much good at expressing herself. She recognized the other women behind Auntie Ah-wang. They—Wangshi, Spring Bough, and the others—were Chencuo women who did their laundry together at the well. She nodded a greeting and then just stood there looking rather stupid.

Auntie Ah-wang completely ignored her. She turned to the offerings on the altar, closely scrutinizing and evaluating each and every item.

"We're here to see what kind of fantastic things you're offering," she said sarcastically.

"Wow! A whole pig's head! This neighborhood's never seen an offering like that before," Spring Bough said enviously, her voice as shrill as ever.

Wangshi and a couple of the other women walked up and made little clucking noises of approval.

Lin Shi, feeling quite proud of herself, demurred: "It's nothing. It's really nothing."

"If you're the butcher you can offer the whole pig if you want to." It was Auntie Ah-wang again. "Now, I'm not one to pick on people, but I can't imagine anyone only offering up five or six dishes on a big festival like this. If you're going to have one of the three sacrificial animals in the center, you're supposed to have at least ten or twenty dishes around it. If you don't even know that, you've sure got a lot to learn."

"Oh!" Lin Shi exclaimed in alarm and confusion. "What happens when the offerings come up short?"

"When orphaned spirits and wandering ghosts don't eat their fill, they come back year after year—they'll never give you any peace." Auntie Ah-wang's voice was cold and grim.

Lin Shi just stood there. The same eerie coldness that had struck her with the sight of Auntie Ah-wang approaching under the scorching sun gripped her again. She was surprised to note that Auntie Ah-wang's voice was different from before: Hoarse and raspy, it sounded like air escaping through a hole cut in her windpipe. Fine perspiration covered Lin Shi's entire body, including her face. Someone beside her touched her arm. It was Wangshi.

"Now, now. Don't be scared," she said. "As long as you're sincere and you've done your best, it doesn't matter how many dishes you put out."

"That may be the case with gods and ancestors, but how much you put out is *very* important to orphaned spirits." Auntie Ah-wang's hoarse, raspy voice cut like a blade worn dull, leaving a bloody mess in its wake. "You ought to be counting your blessings. It's only because of that pig-butcher husband of yours that you can afford to offer up this big fish, all that meat, and—my, my!—even a pig's head."

Now that the women had passed judgment on Lin Shi's offerings, they drifted off to other houses to continue their inspection. Auntie Ah-wang delivered a loud parting shot: "Contentment is a cherished virtue. Pig-Butcher Chen is a good man. 'Amitabha.' The good-hearted will be rewarded. You know, you shouldn't be screaming and carrying on all the time. Someone who didn't know might think that Pig-Butcher Chen was abusing you."

That said, she made a quick exit and caught up with the rest of the women. Lin Shi remained standing by herself for a few moments, but curiosity soon got the better of her, and she decided to tag along with the others. Still worried that stray dogs or cats might get to her food, she kept looking back over her shoulder as she caught up with them.

The women stopped in front of Auntie Ah-wang's house, since it was right next door. Lin Shi arrived just in time to see Wangshi pointing to a platter of food on the altar and remarking disdainfully: "Now don't take me wrong, but is this a platter of noodles? Who on earth would use noodles for an offering?"

"You must be going blind. Either that, or you don't know what you're looking at. Open your eyes and look again." Auntie Ah-wang's dander was up.

Just then the high, shrill voice of Wangshi rent the air: "Those aren't noodles, they're sliced bamboo shoots! Just look at the work that went into that! I've never seen bamboo shoots sliced so fine that they cooked up like noodles."

Harmony, who was standing off to the side, responded warmly but with a touch of embarrassment: "You're too kind. It's nothing special."

Lin Shi hadn't even noticed Harmony's presence until then. This was the same woman who was always trying to be first in everything, Harmony, the shrew. But now, in front of her mother-in-law, Auntie Ah-wang, she stood shrinking off in a corner. The smile on her face showed traces of fear in it and was maintained only with a great deal of effort. Lin Shi recalled the rumors she had heard in recent days—that Harmony was afraid of offending Auntie Ah-wang's hanging ghost. Fearing the ghost might seek her out for revenge, Harmony's attitude toward Auntie Ah-wang had changed radically—she was now the model daughter-in-law, a study in obedience.

The women continued delivering their opinions on the various dishes, repeatedly praising Harmony's handiwork and expressing their envy of Auntie Ah-wang for her luck in being blessed with such a wonderful daughter-in-law. As she listened to the other women, Lin Shi looked long and hard at the makeshift altar of a door plank supported by two rattan chairs. No fewer than twenty or thirty dishes had been laid out. In addition to fish and meat, the altar table was filled with odds and ends like deep-fried vegetable rolls, mock chicken, sun-dried lily pods, some uncooked rice, plus salt and sugar.

"How come there's raw rice and salt and sugar?" asked a mystified Lin Shi.

"So you can have delicacies from land *and* sea," Auntie Ah-wang answered perfunctorily in her raspy voice. Not caring if Lin Shi understood or not, she led the contingent of women to another house nearby.

Lin Shi was afraid to stray too far from her own house, since, unlike Auntie Ah-wang, she didn't have a Harmony at home to keep watch, so she let them walk off without her.

She spent the rest of the afternoon sitting on the stool in her doorway. When she noticed that the three joss sticks she had stuck in the sacrificial animals had nearly burned down, she quickly lit three new ones. This process was repeated several times before the sun started to sink in the west, and the neighbors began burning sacrificial money. In the deepening dusk, tiny bonfires suddenly flared up all around. Once in a while a piece of burning paper would get caught up in a gust of wind and flare briefly, but by the time it fell to the ground, it would already have turned to ashes.

Worried that she had laid out too little food for the orphaned spirits and wandering ghosts, Lin Shi tried to compensate by offering up more prayers, waiting until all her neighbors had taken down their altars before burning her sacrificial money and gathering up her offerings. The dishes of food she took back into the house were cold and covered with incense ash and dust. But that didn't bother her. Since people actually ate incense ash from the temples, why should she worry about a little of it on her food? She hurriedly warmed up the rice and some of the food, set the table, and, as a special gesture, poured a large bowl of wine in readiness for Chen Jiangshui.

Chen Jiangshui still hadn't returned by nightfall. As Lin Shi sat there waiting for him, her eyes fell on the small cloth-wrapped bundle on the altar. She remembered that when Ah-qing brought it over he had said it was a gift from Harmony. Lin Shi had been so preoccupied with observing the rituals all afternoon that she hadn't had time to open it up and see what was inside. It wouldn't hurt to take a peek now, since Chen Jiangshui wasn't home.

She undid the cloth wrapping very carefully. Inside was a folded piece of fabric printed with a pattern of two-inch blue peonies on a coarse white background. The dyeing job left a lot to be desired, for the layers of petals were so jumbled together that she could barely tell that they were supposed to be flowers. And yet she could hardly control the wild pounding of her heart.

A gift from Harmony. She must have meant for Lin Shi to make some clothing out of it. Lin Shi shook it out and wrapped it around herself. Just right for a shirt.

Once she had draped the fabric over her breasts she could hardly bear to take it away. Her gaze fell on the blue cotton shirt she was wearing. It was old and faded by many washings and too small for her womanly body. Tears ran down her cheeks. She quickly wiped them dry with her hand, to keep her new fabric from getting wet.

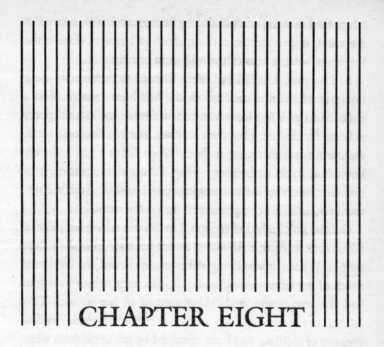

CHAPTER EIGHT

With the festival observance behind them, the people over at Auntie Ah-wang's had had plenty of time to put away all the bowls and dishes, the steaming racks, and the other utensils. But even after several days, Auntie Ah-wang still hadn't come over to sit with Lin Shi. She hadn't been going to the well to do her morning laundry either. One afternoon, when Chen Jiangshui was out, Lin Shi carefully wrapped up the piece of white material printed with blue flowers and went out the back door, heading toward Auntie Ah-wang's by circling around the low, narrow earthen wall in back.

Although it was only the middle of the seventh month, off in the distance where the sea met the sky, early signs of white had already begun to show on the patches of reeds. Long spears of white reed flowers, surrounded by lush green leaves, swayed in the wind, imparting the cooling touch of autumn, despite the lingering, searing heat of the midsummer afternoon.

In days past, Lin Shi had often listened to Auntie Ah-wang boasting of the fine needlework she had been capable of as a child. Most girls just learn how to sew clothes and cloth slippers at home for themselves or their relatives, but Lin Shi could recall Auntie Ah-wang's saying to her: "When I was a girl I already knew how to do embroidery. Why, I'd use thirteen threads of different colors to make a single peony blossom. Even the up-town young ladies complimented me on my work."

On that postfestival afternoon, Lin Shi was taking her piece of fabric over to Auntie Ah-wang to ask her how to make a shirt with it. When she was living in her uncle's house, she had spent much of her time waiting on her invalid aunt, who was sick in bed the year round, and taking care of all her cousins. This had left her no time to even touch a needle and thread. Her few changes of clothing had been obtained by her uncle from who-knows-where, and she almost always went around the house barefoot, for she was allowed the use of a pair of wooden clogs only after she had washed her feet before going to bed at night. She had never owned a pair of cloth slippers, so naturally there was neither the opportunity nor the need for her to learn how to make them—or anything else, for that matter.

That was why on that particular afternoon, instead of taking a nap, she had come looking for Auntie Ah-wang, bundle in hand, hoping that she would finally get a new shirt that would fit her better and be more comfortable, and, she hoped, better looking than the ones she had now. She quickly cut across Auntie Ah-wang's yard and had just reached the back door when she thought she heard someone inside say her name.

She stopped in her tracks and listened closely. Yes, some-one inside was talking about her, someone with a hoarse, raspy voice—it had to be Auntie Ah-wang. "That Lin Shi, she's really . . ." She couldn't make out the rest because of the boisterous laughter that followed. The shrill voice of Spring Bough was the only one she could distinguish. This clearly was not the time for her to knock, so she slipped behind the partially opened back door. She found she could hear much better.

Auntie Ah-wang was still talking: "Take me, for instance. I was prepared to kill myself if that's what it took to show I had the courage of my convictions. That's all a person needs to get by in this world." The tone of her voice became contemptuous: "A person doesn't have to moan and groan all the time to try to make people believe she's having a good time. It's people like that who give all women a bad name. But I guess I'm just wasting my breath talking about her."

More laughter, followed by a good-natured verbal slap: "Auntie Ah-wang, you're not afraid to say anything these days."

"What's there to be afraid of? Everybody knows that all women have the hots for a man's tool . . ."

Again Auntie Ah-wang's voice was drowned out by embarrassed and titillated laughter. The next voice Lin Shi heard was Spring Bough's: "It's not as simple as that. Don't forget that all Pig-Butcher Chen knows how to do is slaughter pigs. Now, how can someone like that afford to keep Lin Shi living in the lap of luxury?"

"You mean you don't even know that?" Wangshi cut in. "Pig-Butcher Chen goes down to the seashore every afternoon to hide in the reeds and gamble with some of the fishermen. I hear he wins just about every hand, and it doesn't matter if he's the bank or the player. That's where his money comes from."

"He's not the only one who gambles. Other people act as the bank, too. That Ah-bian from Niancuo Village, I hear he's the one behind it all." Auntie Ah-wang sounded a bit defensive.

The momentary silence that followed was quickly shattered by the insistent voice of Spring Bough: "You know everything that's going on in the neighborhood. Tell us, is Pig-Butcher Chen really as bad as they say?"

"How could he be?" Auntie Ah-wang demanded. "If he was, he wouldn't have come to my rescue, would he? It's all that greedy Lin Shi's doing. She can't get enough. She wants it day and night. I don't know how anyone can be so shameless! Who ever heard of anyone doing things like that in broad daylight?"

More laughter.

"How do you know what other people do in broad daylight?" someone asked her.

"Oh, come on! She makes so much noise that people three miles away can hear her."

"You sure can't tell by looking at her," commented another.

"That shows how much you know." Lin Shi easily recognized the voice of Wangshi. "A neighbor of my aunt's told me that even before she was married, she used to sit in the doorway and stare at men, and she couldn't keep her eyes off their you-know-what." She giggled.

"So *that's* how it was!" They all seemed to join in on this exclamation of surprise.

Another question—this time it was Wangshi: "Does Pig-Butcher Chen really get all rough and crazy when he does it?"

"There, you see, that shows how well you know him. He's just not that good around people. But he's got a good heart—if he didn't, would he have come to my rescue?" Indignation had crept into Auntie Ah-wang's voice. "So what if he's sort of rough and crude. After all, what do you expect from a butcher? As women, we're supposed to be tolerant and put our husbands above everything else. Who ever heard of anyone raising such a stink over a little pain once in a while! Then, to top it off, she tries to ruin his good name!"

"That's right! That's how it is!" Everywhere there were voices of agreement.

"Take me, for example. I always do what has to be done. When someone tried to assassinate my character, I knew that the only way to prove my virtue was in death. Well, you all saw what happened. The fact that I didn't die proves I was right. Instead of wanting me dead, Heaven let me return to speak the truth. Then take someone like Lin Shi, a woman who really wants to be screwed, but plays hard to get. Not only that . . ."

A shrill voice cut in—it was Spring Bough: "Like wanting to do you-know-what on the very day of her wedding?"

"Like they say, you'll never find a lazy earthworm in a duck pen," Auntie Ah-wang commented with a laugh.

They all hooted their approval.

"Like mother, like daughter." Auntie Ah-wang lowered her voice to heighten the conspiratorial effect. "Did you all know that her mother committed adultery with a soldier about ten years ago, and when Lin Shi's uncle rushed over to catch them in the act, they were coupled together so tight no one could pull them apart?"

"I thought everyone said that he raped her."

"If someone was about to be raped, don't you think she'd run away? Or at least scream and put up a fight? And wouldn't her clothes be torn or something? I'd like to know how someone could be raped without even having her clothes messed up." Auntie Ah-wang's agitation was obvious.

"It's enough to make you split your sides laughing." Her voice was growing shriller by the minute. "Who ever heard of someone sighing and moaning with pleasure while she's being raped?"

"So that's where she learned to scream like that!"

There was a momentary pause, but as the point sank in, the women started to laugh. When their laughter subsided, Auntie

Ah-wang's hoarse, raspy voice started in again: "That's right! You can't get tender shoots from a rotten bamboo stalk. I'm sure her mother never imagined that neglecting her daughter's education when she was a child would be the cause of her own death— you see, the little one ran off to get help while her mother was having the time of her life."

With what felt like an explosion in her head, Lin Shi's scalp began to tingle, and her whole head seemed to swell. Strange chirping noises assaulted her ears as her terror rose, and she was drenched in perspiration. As she began to return to normal, she glanced over at the corner of the yard. A brood of newly hatched ducklings chirped noisily in their bamboo coop. In her confusion she thought she heard the wind whistling across the vast mudflats. The veins above her temples throbbed and pulsated. Gradually the voices of the women began to filter through again: " . . . daughter following in her mother's footsteps. What's the difference between a woman like that and those bitches in Backstreet?"

"I know what you mean. Look at her, all by herself and putting on all those airs. She ought to be thankful that she's got no inlaws to take care of, but no, all she does is lie around and let the house go to pot while she eats and sleeps the day away. That is, except for the times when she rolls over and lets her man . . ."

"Well, I hear she's not content with just fooling around in the daytime, either, but even likes to try it in different places—anywhere but in the bedroom . . . hee-hee."

"Just like her mother. She had the gall to fool around with that soldier right in the main hall of the ancestral temple, not giving a damn if the God of Thunder struck her dead right on the spot. That's what I call shameless!"

Lin Shi stood there, no longer able to distinguish one voice from another. There was just one mixed jumble of raucous talk and laughter pouring out of the room. Once in a while a random recognizable word or sentence penetrated her head and filled her ears, reverberating so violently it sounded like a long shrill shriek. Eventually she became aware of the harsh rays of the sun—they were so blindingly hot they caused an earth-spinning dizziness.

She must have walked home, but for the life of her, she couldn't remember how or when. It wasn't until she felt a stinging slap from Chen Jiangshui that she became aware that dusk had fallen; she had been sitting in one of the rattan chairs in the living room, oblivious to the passage of time. Her shirt was drenched with sweat, the wet spots front and back so large she could have wrung the water out of them. The cloth-wrapped bundle was still in her hand. But now it struck fear in her heart—she jumped to her feet and flung it to the ground. It landed a short distance in front of her and came undone, exposing the white cloth printed with blue peonies. A corner of it was wet with perspiration, and a few of the blue peonies had taken on a slightly pink cast, as though splattered with blood, traces of which remained despite attempts to remove them.

Lin Shi prepared dinner as usual while Chen Jiangshui sat waiting at the table, shouting all manner of filthy, insulting curses at her. He started to drink heavily. By the time dinner was over, his face showed how very drunk he was. His brows, which had always been puffy, were now smeared with a glossy ruddiness, and his face was covered with greasy sweat, partly because of the inner heat generated by the wine and partly because of the stuffy room. His whole face seemed to have swelled up, appearing fatter and rounder than usual.

Leering, he grabbed hold of Lin Shi, reaching down with one hand and feeling between her legs. When he found that the pad was missing, he eagerly pinned her on the dirt floor of the living room. At first she tried desperately to free herself, but when she saw that escape was impossible, she stopped struggling and, from start to finish, kept her mouth tightly shut, not making a single sound.

It took Chen Jiangshui a while to discover that Lin Shi wasn't screaming this time, but when he did, he was rougher with her than ever. Yet no matter what he did, she didn't make a sound. When the pain became nearly unbearable, she bit down on her lower lip so hard that she broke the skin, and blood seeped into her mouth—salty, brackish blood.

Thanks to the fact that he was very drunk, Chen Jiangshui went ahead and finished instead of keeping up the punishment. He rolled off her and went to sleep. Lin Shi curled up into a ball, hugging herself tightly and whimpering like a wounded animal. The wails inside her stuck in her throat. Using all her willpower to force back the air that wanted so badly to escape, she actually stopped breathing momentarily a number of times, her face turning bright red, her throat aching unbearably, as though she were being strangled.

It was a summer night soon after the fifteenth of the month. No wind. A bright moon, fresh night breezes. Sea breezes gently stroked the sleeping beach, the distant sound of the shifting tide faded in and out amid the surrounding stillness.

On the morning of the following day, Lin Shi looked at herself in an old cracked mirror she had found. She discovered that her lower lip and her jaw were badly swollen and that a night of weeping had reduced her eyes to tiny slits.

Laboriously she finished the simple task of tidying up the house, then put the basket full of laundry on the bed. But instead of going over to the well to wash clothes, she sat in the rattan chair and absently watched the sun climb until it was directly overhead. Realizing that Chen Jiangshui would be returning soon, she moved the chair inside and crouched down in a corner of the kitchen.

Chen Jiangshui brought a big piece of meat home with him, and Lin Shi managed to compose herself enough to cook it for lunch. After the food was on the table, she took a big bite without thinking. When the salty meat came in contact with her lower lip, she experienced a stabbing pain that seemed to pierce her very heart, hurting so much she couldn't hold back the tears.

After lunch, Chen Jiangshui was on his way out, as usual, when Lin Shi looked up and asked faintly after a momentary hesitation: "Where are you going?"

"Huh? Who are you to ask me where I'm going?" he asked, more out of surprise and curiosity than anger.

"They say you go out to gamble." The words did not come easily. "People who prey on others die without heirs."

Cheng Jiangshui roared with laughter.

"I don't steal from them and I don't hold them up. No one forces them to come—they gamble because they want to."

"Could you stop going?" Lin Shi began timorously, gradually becoming somewhat more resolute. "Then people wouldn't gossip about you.

"I'll stay with you, no matter how difficult it gets," she added naively.

That did it—Chen Jiangshui's temper exploded. His face underwent a complete transformation as he turned on her savagely: "I provide you with food and a roof over your head. If you're not satisfied and think you can interfere in my affairs," he threatened through clenched teeth, "you've got another think coming. You're lucky I'm letting you off with just a warning this time."

Lin Shi quickly lowered her head and kept her mouth shut.

She spent that afternoon in the rattan chair by the door, napping where she sat whenever she felt drowsy. She went into the bedroom several times to lie down, but found it impossible to sleep. As soon as she shut her eyes, her mind was flooded with all kinds of strange dreams. Her eyelids were so heavy she couldn't open them, no matter how she tried. Somehow she managed to bolt out of the room, in a terrible fright, and sit back down in the rattan chair, as if to prove to herself that she hadn't really taken a nap. She stayed there watching the bright summer sun until three or four o'clock, when she picked up her laundry basket and headed for the well.

The water that had accumulated on the granite around the base of the well from the morning wash had long since dried up after a day of blistering heat. Now the sunlight that was reflected off the ground had a grayish sheen to it. Lin Shi had walked barefoot up the dirt road, and the soles of her feet were already burning from the heat. The sight of the gray granite stones made her feel apprehensive, but she knew she had to cross the paved area if she was going to draw any water from the well.

Even after steeling herself for the shock she knew was coming, she yelped in spite of herself when her feet actually touched the stone paving. Moving quickly on the balls of her feet, she managed to negotiate the distance to the edge of the well. Hopping from one foot to the other, she lowered the bucket into the well, brought it right back up, and poured the first bucketful of water onto the ground where she was standing. The water that felt cool when it first touched her feet was quickly heated by the hot granite surface. But at least now she could stand the heat, if only barely.

By the time she had drawn enough water to wash her laundry, the clothes she was wearing were so soaked with perspiration they stuck to her body. The area around the well didn't offer any shade from the blistering heat of the July afternoon, and Lin Shi was drenched with sweat from just crouching in the sun. Once she actually began to scrub the clothes, the sweat poured off her like rain. By the time she finished the laundry, her mouth was as dry as a bone. She got to her feet to return home. But suddenly everything blurred—she stumbled and fell face down, striking her head on a corner of the wooden tub with a dull thud.

Now she knew why the women went to the well so early in the morning to do their laundry. Yet even with the knowledge that doing her laundry in the hot afternoon sun was doubly difficult, she still went to the well every afternoon. When she left the house, she kept her head down and walked as fast as she could for fear that she might run into someone she knew. On those occasions when she saw someone coming her way whom she thought she recognized, she quickly slipped into a side street or an alley, and if it was too late to take any evasive action, then she just lowered her head and pretended she didn't see the person.

Evading Chen Jiangshui, on the other hand, wasn't that easy. But Lin Shi was determined not to scream and moan anymore, and that, of course, drove him into a wild fury. He hit, he choked, he pinched, he prolonged the time he was inside her, but she just gritted her teeth and bore it all in silence—except for the panting hisses that escaped from between her teeth, like the gasps of a tiny animal in the throes of death.

On those occasions when it was nearly more than she could bear, she would let out low mournful groans, which reverberated in her mouth, sorrowful and dreadful to hear.

She had tried resisting, of course. No matter how Chen Jiangshui abused her, eventually he would stop and, for a brief moment, be concerned only with his frantic movements as he straddled her. Once, when he was least expecting it, Lin Shi shoved him off her, then rolled off the bed, and, finding no place to hide in the house, threw open the door and ran outside. There in the bright moonlight, directly ahead of her, was Auntie Ah-wang, standing in the gateway to their yard.

Auntie Ah-wang's dark pants were hardly visible in the darkness of night, but her dingy white shirt reflected the moonlight, giving off a shimmering, white aura that was quite distinct. Bolting out the door, all Lin Shi saw was a white torso suspended in the dim light. A piteous cry escaped from her lips, her legs turned to rubber, and she collapsed to the ground.

When she got her bearings again, she realized that it was Auntie Ah-wang. She looked up. The old woman was still standing there, her head held high, her gray hair gathered into a neat, tight bun, her white shirt smooth and unwrinkled. She was as neat as a pin—nothing was out of place. There was a strong and unmistakable look of contempt on her upraised face. When she saw Lin Shi straightening up, she grunted meaningfully, turned, and headed home at an unhurried pace.

Lin Shi knew only too well that Chen Jiangshui was waiting for her behind the door, and still she crawled back to the house on all fours. The moment she was in the room, he bolted the door behind her and aimed a kick in the direction of her stomach. At that very moment a dim recollection came to her. A long time ago, just after Chen Jiangshui had had his way with her, she had opened the door to go outside, where she had spotted Auntie Ah-wang at the low earthen wall separating the two houses, not sure whether she was coming or going.

Auntie Ah-wang must have been secretly watching her and Chen Jiangshui all this time, Lin Shi thought, just before she was overcome by a wave of pain. Her stomach felt as though it were a boiling mass, as though all her blood were about to gush forth. Then everything went black and she lost consciousness.

She came to, choking on wine. Seeing that she had regained

consciousness, Chen Jiangshui left her on the floor and went to bed. Lin Shi was too weak to get up. Fearful of another assault from Chen Jiangshui, she spent the night on the floor. Exhausted, she fell into a fitful sleep. Throughout the unusually cold summer night, she shivered on the damp dirt floor. In the morning she found that she was hot and dry all over, that her head felt as though it weighed a ton. She sat up with difficulty.

Since Chen Jiangshui was out, she crawled into bed and fell into a troubled sleep. It was already past noon when she woke up. Chen Jiangshui hadn't returned, so she slept on, like someone drugged, occasionally regaining consciousness briefly. Night followed, then gave way to day. She had no idea how long she had lain there or whether Chen Jiangshui had been home at all.

The next time she regained consciousness, she was being shaken awake. She lay with her eyes open for a long while before she could make out that it was Ah-qing from next door.

"Water," she said with difficulty, not even sure if any sound emerged. "Give me some water."

Ah-qing touched her forehead. She felt a pair of large, thick, and very cool hands descend on her, and she closed her eyes again, feeling very, very comfortable. Then she felt someone lift up her head and place a bowl of water to her lips. She sipped the water slowly, again and again, until she fell into a heavy sleep again.

This time dreams came. Lin Shi's mother was all dressed in red. Her legs were bound with several coils of a long, thick rope. Stretching her arms out toward her daughter, she said over and over: "Ah-shi, I'm hungry, I'm hungry, I'm hungry . . . go beg some food for me, I'm hungry, I'm hungry."

Lin Shi discovered that she couldn't move a muscle, but she didn't know why. Momentary confusion followed. Unable to wait any longer, her mother plunged her hands into her own abdomen, fished out a mass of bloody entrails, and hungrily shoved them into her mouth, giggling as she said: "I've got nothing to eat. Just this sweet-potato mash."

Lin Shi fought to wake up. She gradually became aware that she had only been dreaming, but she couldn't open her eyes, as though she were under a spell. Someone was shaking her and calling her name: "Lin Shi, Lin Shi, you've got to come back. Come back . . ."

Fully awake, she forced her eyes open and saw Ah-qing holding a bowl to her lips. Instinctively, she opened her mouth and began to take small sips. Although she had a hazy notion that it must have been some sort of medicine, she didn't taste the bitterness until the last few swallows.

Suddenly someone swept the bowl aside. It was Chen Jiangshui, drunk again by the look of his bright red face. He grabbed Ah-qing by the collar.

"What the fuck are you trying to do to my wife?" he shouted. "You fucker!"

"She's sick. She's hot all over. I went out and got her some herbal medicine," Ah-qing said calmly.

"You fucking phony! I know what's on your mind. Fuck your mother! Up your mother's old cunt!"

"I won't try to reason with you while you're drunk." Ah-qing wrenched free of Chen Jiangshui's hold and turned to go. Chen Jiangshui grabbed his butcher knife from the Eight-Immortals table and chased after him. "You're not leaving till I get the whole story!"

"You came to my mother's aid once, so I'm not going to argue with you." Ah-qing quickly backed out the door. "My mother found out that Lin Shi had taken sick and told me to come over. She said I had to come to her aid, that she had to repay a debt. I wasn't supposed to say anything, but you give me no choice."

Just before he left, he added with a solemn expression on his face: "I'm sure you've heard this, too: If you don't hold on to the merits you've accumulated, the day may come when you have none left."

Lin Shi, watching Ah-qing's departing figure, was suddenly aware that night had long since fallen.

CHAPTER NINE

After her illness, Lin Shi was her former gaunt self. She now also seemed to be in a state of constant fear. As though she were trying to hide from something, she began hunching over in an attempt to make herself as small as possible. She still waited until well past noon before making her timid, furtive daily trips to the well to do her laundry. Taking only the small side streets, her eyes darted watchfully here and there. With her skin deeply tanned by constant exposure to the sun, she had the shriveled appearance of a wind-dried shrimp.

Chen Jiangshui had taken to not coming home for several days in a row. Occasionally Lin Shi would overhear gossip that he was staying with Golden Flower in Backstreet, but the news didn't bother her in the slightest. As long as she didn't have to worry about the supply of rice and sweet-potato mash in her bin, she was glad that he stayed away. It meant that much less abuse and degradation for her to endure.

Each day Lin Shi took her rattan chair and sat in the doorway, apparently not so much to watch the passersby as to show everyone that she hadn't taken up the slothful habit of napping during the day. Eventually this became a daily ritual: She would bring her chair over and sit in the doorway until the sun had started sinking in the west. Then she would pick up her laundry basket and head for the well.

This routine remained unchanged until Lin Shi began raising a brood of ducklings. No one knew why she suddenly took it into her head to raise ducklings, but one day she showed up bright and early in front of the Chencuo temple, where she told one of the peddlers that she wanted to buy some ducklings.

"I want ten ducklings," she said, "all females. Once they start laying, I'll have ten eggs a day."

The peddler, who had come into town from a farm near Lucheng, looked at Lin Shi with amusement.

"If you don't have a male to fertilize the eggs, they won't hatch," he said with a laugh. "Then what's the point in having so many eggs?"

Oh! Lin Shi let this news sink in.

"I didn't know eggs had to be fertilized," she said haltingly. "I just want to sell some eggs for enough money to buy rice and sweet-potato mash. Does it make any difference if they're fertilized or not?"

As the peddler watched Lin Shi wrestle with this problem, he saw a look of dismay spread across her face and decided to stop teasing her. One by one he picked up the fuzzy yellow ducklings, took a good look under their tails, and set ten of them off to one side.

"I think you ought to buy six females and four males. When the males are grown, you can sell them as poultry and use that money to buy your rice."

Lin Shi groped around in her jacket pocket for what seemed like an eternity. After ripping out a row of stitches, she fished out a small packet wrapped in oil-paper, which, when unwrapped, was about the size of her palm. There were still remnants of the black ointment inside, and bits of it, hardened and cracked, clung to the copper coins that had been wrapped in the packet. As she rubbed the coins, the ointment peeled off in flakes.

She very carefully counted out the number of coins the duck peddler asked for, then counted them again and again before handing them over to him. She put the few remaining coins back into the oil-paper, wrapped them tightly, and put them back into her jacket pocket. Then she picked up the cageful of ducklings and walked off.

As she was leaving the marketplace, a middle-aged woman who was walking toward her, a stranger, greeted her in a friendly way and asked where she had bought the ducklings. Lin Shi pointed the duck-peddler out to her, but when the woman saw who it was she frowned and gave Lin Shi some friendly advice: "Don't be taken in by that no-account duck-peddler. He's known for passing off male ducks for females, so don't you buy the wrong ones."

Lin Shi panicked. Her heart felt as though it were being squeezed, stifling and suffocating her unbearably. It began to pound madly. Not having the nerve to turn back to even look at the duck-peddler, she rushed off, clutching the cage with the ducklings inside, avoiding the main roads and keeping to the alleys as much as possible, finally arriving home after a great deal of unnecessary walking.

She sat there fretting the whole afternoon over the possibility that her ducklings were males, which would never lay eggs. She turned them all over to check them out, but their sex remained a mystery to her. All of a sudden she remembered what the duck-peddler had told her about the male ducks, that they could be sold as poultry. That thought was enough to put her in a happy mood. She ran off to look for something to feed the ducklings, which by now were chirping loudly.

From then on, whenever she had the time, Lin Shi would go out into the fields or over to the edge of the stream to search out earthworms, insects, snails, and other things that she could feed to the ducklings. The sight of her little ducklings fighting over the food and shedding their yellow down for pointed, stiff new feathers—some short, some long—always brought a smile to her face.

The weather gradually turned cool. Off in the distance, near the seashore, the patches of reeds had sprouted spears topped by grayish white flowers, so that the azure blue of the clear, crisp autumn sky was dotted by puffs of fluffy white. There was an aura of calm serenity. Except for the nights, that is, when the autumn winds gathered strength and tumbled across the vast deserted surface of the sandy, pebble-covered beach, like waves of sound, each one louder than the one before.

Lin Shi was worried that the ducklings would catch cold in their cage, so she brought in some sheaves of straw from the field to weave a screen to keep out the wind. During Chen Jiang-shui's prolonged absences from home, periods when no rice was brought into the house, Lin Shi only managed to eat now and then. But she spent long hours beside her ducklings, watching them grow and looking forward to the time when the females would start laying. Even if there weren't six females, she reasoned, even if the duck-peddler *had* tricked her, there should still be four or five egg-layers in the bunch.

But it was not in the cards for Lin Shi to see the day when her ducks would be grown and she could tell how many of them were egg-laying females and how many were males that could be sold as poultry.

For the longest time Chen Jiangshui came home only rarely, but he always brought food with him, and, naturally, he always wanted Lin Shi. For her part, she never so much as whimpered, no matter what he did. Chen Jiangshui tried his best to make her scream every single time, prolonging his tormentings as much as possible. But he wasn't home all that much, which meant that his demands weren't as incessant as they had been in the past. True, Lin Shi no longer had her occasional fish and meat and she often went hungry, but without Chen Jiangshui's constant molesting, there was far less to complain about now. Besides, she could pin her hopes on her female ducks, which would lay the eggs that would insure her forever against the hunger she so dreaded.

One cool night in autumn, when Lin Shi was in bed sound asleep, Chen Jiangshui began pounding on the door with all his might. Lin Shi could see that his face was already flushed with wine and that he was holding a bottle in his hand. Fearing that she was in for more tormenting and, most likely, a beating, she scurried off to one side after opening the door for him, putting as much distance as possible between them.

But Chen Jiangshui hadn't taken more than a couple of steps into the house when he stumbled over the cage filled with ducklings. Lin Shi had been worried that they might catch cold at night now that the weather was turning cool, so she had brought the cage inside and put it on the bed of straw she had laid out in the living room. Chen Jiangshui, already tipsy from the wine, stumbled over the cage in the darkness and nearly lost his footing altogether. As he was fighting to maintain his balance, the bottle slipped from his grasp and fell heavily to the floor, smashing to pieces.

"What the hell's going on!" he bellowed with rage. "Have you got a lover you're trying to hide in the house?"

"It's, it's just some ducklings."

"Liar! I don't believe you."

He went up and snatched the lid off the cage. The frantic duck-lings, quacking for all they were worth, crowded into a corner of the cage. Chen Jiangshui violently slammed the lid back on, catching one of the slow-moving ducklings by its leg. It cried pitifully as it struggled to free itself, but its plight failed to move Chen Jiangshui.

"Ducks stink to high heaven!" he shouted venomously at Lin Shi. "You stinking whore, are you trying to suffocate me by rais-ing ducks in the house?"

Lin Shi, whose attention was riveted on the trapped duckling, didn't answer. Her only thought was to go to the duckling's res-cue, but Chen Jiangshui was next to the cage. Standing there anxiously, Lin Shi was plagued by a single fear: Her duckling was probably going to be lame.

Lin Shi's inattentiveness increased Chen Jiangshui's anger. He reeled and slapped her hard.

"What are you raising these ducks for?"

"Ducks lay eggs. We can sell them and use the money to buy rice," she answered without giving it any thought.

"So, you think I don't feed you enough, huh? You want to raise ducks so you can have more to eat, eh?" Chen Jiangshui asked in icy tones.

"Sometimes you don't bring any rice home, and I . . ."

Without waiting for her to finish, he reached behind him and picked up his butcher knife. Lin Shi was terrified, thinking that he was going to use it on her, and she backed away in panic. But he thrust his hand into the cage and began hacking away in a frenzy, using so much force that he broke the bamboo cage in a number of places. The ducklings cried pitifully at first, but before long, all was silence. Chen Jiangshui withdrew his hand. The bright, clear light of the autumn moon streaming in through the door revealed a dark red stain running from his palm to his elbow. The fresh, uncongealed blood dripped slowly down his raised arm.

With a scream Lin Shi rushed over and lifted up the cover. There, scattered all over the bed of straw, were the broken carcasses of her ducklings—heads, bodies, feet, necks—all oozing blood.

When Chen Jiangshui saw the dismembered bodies he shivered all over. How could that have happened, he wondered—how could he have made such a chaotic, gory mess, instead of the clean, neat cuts he made when he butchered the pigs? An episode from the past suddenly flashed into his mind.

He had only been working in the slaughterhouse a short time. Since he was still quite young and inexperienced with a knife, he mainly did odd jobs like removing bristles from the pigs' skin and cleaning their organs and intestines. One day some men with a carrying pole brought in a sow, which the owner said was too sick to stand up by itself. If it wasn't slaughtered right away it might be too late.

The sow was nothing but skin and bones, except, that is, for its belly, which hung nearly to the ground when the animal finally managed to stagger to its feet. The people in the slaughterhouse began to talk among themselves, some of them saying that the sow had swine fever. No one was willing to kill a diseased pig, and the butcher in charge kept his mouth shut.

The owner insisted that the sow be slaughtered at once, that it would never last the night. Just then, in order to show off his abilities and improve his chances of getting ahead, Chen Jiangshui volunteered for the job.

Everything proceeded normally, including the ritual of smearing blood on the animal's mouth and the ceremonial removal of the hair. The sow's strength was virtually exhausted, so when Chen grasped its snout before plunging his knife into its gullet to let its blood, it didn't put up any struggle at all, making it possible for Chen to accomplish his job without a hitch. The extraordinarily sad look he thought he saw in the sow's eyes he quickly dismissed as a figment of his imagination.

But then, when the belly was sliced open, they saw a huge lump entangled in the bloody mess. It nearly filled the abdominal cavity.

"Oh no!" someone cried out in dismay. "You've killed a pregnant sow that was just about to deliver."

Chen Jiangshui, who had yet to feel a sense of alarm, sliced open the bloody mass. Inside, lying one next to the other in a neat row, were eight fully formed baby pigs, all covered with blood. Eight tiny, hairless animals, their soft bodies still warm, their eyes tightly closed. Everyone knew that they would not survive.

The destruction of the womb, the source of all life under heaven, caused Chen Jiangshui to pass the next several days and nights in terror—the sight of those bloody, fully formed but aborted lives always in front of his eyes. People in the slaughterhouse were saying that when an expectant sow was killed, her piglets would demand their right to life from the person responsible, who was thus fated to die a horrible death. Instructed by the slaughterhouse assistants, Chen Jiangshui prepared three sacrificial animals and a large quantity of paper money as offerings. He also prayed for the baby pigs' reincarnation. But even that didn't completely purge his heart of guilt, or of the unclean feeling that had come from his contact with a pregnant womb.

With the passage of time, however, it all faded into history. Significantly, he suffered no retribution. Occasionally he would be reminded of this incident, but all that remained was the vivid image of that huge round lump in the abdomen, its dull, flesh-colored surface covered with crisscrossing purplish veins. And, of course, those globs of blood.

In all the years since, butchering pigs had remained a clean experience for him. Increasingly expert technique had transformed every aspect of his work into a performance. The letting of blood took only a single downward stroke, and the blood never so much as touched his hands. The opening of the abdomen took only a single slash, and not a drop of blood dripped from the exposed flesh. The organs and intestines that tumbled out were gray in color, the heart and liver were a clean, purplish red; they were never marred by a single cut, nor was there any blood on them.

And yet this time, in killing just a few ducklings, he had created a grisly mess of blood and gore. As he raised his bloody hand, his fear turned to anger—an unreasonable, nameless, mounting fury that he could not explain, let alone control. In that brief moment, all he wanted to do was slash out with his knife, to kill something. But then his gaze fell upon the carcasses of the ducklings again, and a genuine fear rose in him. He threw down his butcher knife and fell to his knees.

Always there had been this surge of energy, gathering and then rising from his abdominal region. At first he had needed it, carefully cultivating and storing it for that ultimate moment when his butcher knife descended, so that it would plunge unerringly into the gullet of the struggling, squealing animal; then, after the bright red blood had spurted out of the wound, and he knew that the force had brought this life to an end, he had to be able to once again refocus that same force in order to plunge his knife into the gullet of yet another living animal and end its life, too. Thus the cycle repeated itself, nonstop, so that with each passing day and each passing month, he had destroyed, one after another, countless living, breathing lives.

After years of constant practice, there was no longer any mystery as to how he bred and nurtured this force so that it worked for him, and he was hardly conscious of it. Of all the countless times he had wielded his knife, he could recall only once when he was aware of the careful accumulation of the force that had given him the nerve to plunge in his knife, and that was the time he had killed the sow with the eight piglets in its womb, an incident that was indelibly etched in his memory. If it hadn't been for this episode with the ducklings, he probably would not have been reminded of the existence of this force and its power over him.

For the first time in his life, Chen Jiangshui realized, however vaguely, that this drive to kill, which was so necessary in his profession, had merged into his life and had become an integral part of it. Now, even when he wasn't on the job, it could be summoned with a mere thought, producing actions and consequences over which he had absolutely no control.

This time he had slaughtered a bunch of ducklings. What would it be the next time? He wondered. A wave of terror overwhelmed him. Still slightly drunk, he opened his mouth wide and gave himself over to loud wailing.

Meanwhile, Lin Shi, who had rushed over to lift up the lid of the cage, found the dismembered carcasses scattered about inside. Surprisingly, she just stood there without making a sound. She waited until Chen Jiangshui had stopped wailing and had crawled off to the bedroom, then continued waiting until she heard his snores before stirring herself. After fetching a broom and dustpan from the backyard, she swept up all the straw and the broken body parts, carried them outside, and walked toward the distant horizon.

The patches of reeds were farther away than she had expected.

After walking for a while, all she could see under the clear autumn moon was a long shadow where the sky met the sea. The autumn winds chilled the night air, and all over the wide expanse under the deserted sky, shadows lurked. She heard an occasional cry from an animal, but it was immediately swallowed up in the surrounding silence. Apparently oblivious to everything around her, she just kept walking until she grew tired. Then she dumped the mixture of broken carcasses and straw into a patch of waist-high grass and turned back, dustpan in hand.

Now that she no longer had to feed the ducklings, Lin Shi resumed her daily routine of moving her rattan chair over to the doorway and sitting there with a blank stare. Her neighbors assumed that she would greet them when they passed by, but she stared right through them.

Most of the time Lin Shi just sat there the whole afternoon. She not only stopped going to the well to do her laundry, but often forgot all about dinner. It usually wasn't until Chen Jiangshui returned home, when the sky had already grown dark, that she finally got up to cook dinner.

The stovetop, long in need of a cleaning, was coated with a film of grease, and in one corner of the stove there was a cobweb, which was adorned with the leg of a fly that had been eaten by a spider. The place was covered with dust, but Lin Shi didn't seem to notice. She would just throw a quick, simple meal together, then crouch down beside the stove deep in thought about something or other. She neither washed nor changed her blue cotton blouse for days on end. There were grimy rings around the collar and the sleeves, and there was a stain near her breast where she had spilled some soup; whenever she rested her head on her chest, the stain looked like a shadow cast by her gaunt, pointed jaw.

The stove was the only warm spot in the house. Crouched next to it, she could still feel traces of heat, like a warm embrace, in the autumn air chilled by the sea breezes. Even after she had finished cooking, she would continue crouching there, not getting to her feet until Chen Jiangshui began shouting for his dinner.

Chen Jiangshui had resumed coming home every day at the same time, and he had stopped shouting at her and beating her so much. Even when he was taking her, he wasn't as brutal as he had been before. Now Lin Shi just bore it like a person in a trance, as though she no longer felt anything. She didn't even have to clench her teeth to keep herself from crying out.

The weather really began to turn cold. Even in the daytime, the chilly, gusty wind blowing in from the distant horizon turned dry and blustery, churning and sweeping up the yellow sand from the beach. Whipping by, it stung faces and hands already numbed by the bitter cold.

Lin Shi's indifference finally brought Chen Jiangshui's wrath down upon her. It happened when she accidentally dropped a plateful of three-layered stew, soaked in soy sauce. Chen Jiangshui, who apparently could restrain himself no longer, raised his hand and slapped her across the face.

"Just look at the way you waste food! And you were talking about raising ducks in order to buy food!"

He stomped his foot and screamed at her, but she just stood there, confused but no longer afraid. That infuriated him even more, and his temper, long dormant, drove him to flip over the table with a violent heave, sending the bowls, chopsticks, and a pot of rice porridge crashing to the floor.

"Since you're so clever," he said savagely as he stormed out the door, "from now on you can feed yourself. My rice isn't good enough for you."

True to his threat, from then on Chen Jiangshui kept the rice, sweet-potato mash, and other foodstuffs locked up in the cupboard, doling out a small quantity at each meal for Lin Shi to prepare. After she had cooked it for him, not only would he not share it with her, but he would make her stand beside the table and wait on him, tormenting her by ordering: "Fill my rice-bowl!"

Looking on with helpless longing, she filled his bowl with rice. He sent it crashing to the table with a sweep of his hand.

"What do you think I am, a 'starving ghost'?" he demanded angrily. "What's the idea of putting so much in there? You trying to get me bloated, or what?"

Lin Shi reluctantly took it back and wistfully scooped some of the rice back into the pot. Then, fearing there was still too much in the bowl, she resolutely scooped out a little more. How her heart ached!

When the rice was served to him, Chen Jiangshui wolfed it down in two or three mouthfuls, with great relish, then taunted her: "Aren't you hungry? Wouldn't you like a little of this?"

Lin Shi stared at the gleaming white rice and swallowed over and over.

"When whores want to eat, they have to work. You willing to work?"

"Doing what?" Lin Shi asked, hesitantly, timidly.

"You just moan a few times, like before, and if I find it satisfactory, well, I'll reward you with a bowl of rice."

Lin Shi fearfully took a couple of steps backwards. She looked at the rice. With great difficulty, she shook her head.

Despite Chen Jiangshui's threats and efforts to tempt her with food, Lin Shi steadfastly refused to give in. His only recourse was to intensify his abuse, to further torment her, but nothing he did succeeded in making her cry out. Several days passed, but Lin Shi, who hadn't eaten at all, appeared none the worse because of it. She still wandered dazedly around the house all day long, sitting first in one spot, then switching to another, crouching first beside the stove, then in the bedroom. It didn't take Chen Jiangshui long to discover that she was eating on the sly.

Always on the alert, she carefully surveyed the area, making sure that Chen Jiangshui was still in the other room before lifting up the lid of the pot to check on the big piece of meat in the bubbling soup, then at the big ball of rice. She turned around and took another look, then scooped up the piece of meat with a spoon and shoved it into her mouth. *Ouch! Too hot!* She spat it out into her hand, then crouched down and made as though she were stoking the fire with some pieces of firewood as she ate. She chewed and she swallowed, and by the time she had gotten slowly to her feet, it was gone. One last careful glance around the room assured her that Chen Jiangshui still hadn't come out of the other room.

Even though her only opportunities to eat came while the food was being prepared on the stove, Lin Shi still managed to get enough each time—usually not entirely cooked—since Chen Jiangshui had no idea how much rice it took to make a meal.

He started getting suspicious when he noticed that Lin Shi didn't look at all like a woman who was slowly starving. By being just a little more observant, he finally caught her red-handed. He hated her for refusing to beg for mercy or plead with him for a bowl of rice, and he hated her for having the guts to steal food. His anger really erupted this time. He gave her a brutal beating and stopped eating at home altogether. Instead he returned to his bachelor routine—he began eating all his meals at the noodle stand in Chencuo's marketplace, having no intention of bringing any more food home.

Over the first few days, Lin Shi searched high and low, hoping to turn up something to eat. In the back of the cupboard she found some long forgotten packages of noodles. They were covered with gray-green spots the size of copper coins and had begun to sprout fine hairs a half-inch or so in length, making them look like the rotting faces of legendary ghosts. She picked off the green spots and rinsed the noodles several times in water, then cooked and ate them.

When she had eaten them all, she finally remembered—those were the noodles Ah-qing had given them for the sacrifice, along with the pig's feet, in appreciation for their having saved Auntie Ah-wang. Then she recalled an all-but-forgotten episode, which gave rise to a superstitious fear in her heart.

It was the year her father had died and they had been thrown out of their house by her uncle. Her mother, who had been unable to find work doing laundry, managed only an occasional cleaning job for some of the townspeople in Lucheng. So they had passed most of their days in hunger.

Mother had instructed her that no matter how hungry they got they were never to eat the sacrificial food people set up in out-of-the-way places. These sacrifices usually consisted of a bowl of rice and a small dish of food, with three joss sticks stuck in the rice. According to Mother, sacrifices like these were usually offerings of people who were tormented by evil spirits. In order to rid themselves of bad luck, they had to find some dark corner and set up an anonymous sacrifice. Ordinary people would be plagued by the evil spirits if they so much as looked at these sacrifices, so whenever they happened across one by accident, they had to quickly spit in the direction of the sacrifice.

But hunger can win out over any fear. Ultimately, one day, Lin Shi removed the burned-down joss sticks from a ricebowl and ate the rice along with a piece of fatty pork that had been placed on the small dish. The rice looked nice and gleaming white on the surface, but when she got down to the middle she found it was all gooey and stuck together. Even though she had remembered to spit on the ground some ten or twelve times before taking a single bite, she still got the runs and started throwing up not long after she returned home. She also ran a fever and was visited by demons and monsters with green-and-red faces worming their way into her mouth, one after another.

Mother said she nearly died that time. But Lin Shi never dared tell her what had actually caused the illness, for she was afraid that as soon as she divulged it, even more long-tongued, fang-toothed, bulging-eyed demons would come after her.

Lin Shi waited for retribution to come for having eaten the noodles intended for the hanging ghost, just as it had that time before. After a day had gone by without any signs, she was filled with dread. In spite of herself, she couldn't help thinking about all those strands of noodles, each of them attached to the purple tongue of a hanging ghost, and all of them now resting in her stomach, jabbering back and forth, just waiting to go into action.

Burdened by her own fears, Lin Shi forcefully resisted Chen Jiangshui's demands. She was afraid that once he mounted her, his movements would disturb the long tongues of the hanging ghosts in her stomach. Besides, since he hadn't brought food home for such a long time, she was no longer obliged to submit to him. First she kept her thighs tightly closed, not allowing him to enter her. Then, when she was finally overcome by his superior strength, she kept her eyes open for any opportunity to hit, bite, or kick the body of the man on top of her, especially when he was in the throes of his final jerking motions and she had a chance to struggle free. Naturally, Chen Jiangshui always retaliated against her struggles with even more severe beatings.

When the leftover food inside the house and the vegetables in the plot outside were all gone, Lin Shi had no more strength to resist, and she once again had to suffer the pangs of hunger.

This hunger came swiftly, like an invasion. It was already more than she could bear though she had missed only two or three meals. The emptiness inside her spread until her stomach seemed to be right up against her backbone. Her body, wracked by intense pain, lacked the strength to stand. A sticky, bitter fluid began dribbling from her mouth.

Finally, one evening, after the fishing folk had returned from the sea, Lin Shi emerged from her house and, following a stone-paved road that ran through Chencuo, stopped at each door along the way to ask if the people there had any work for her to do.

"Kind Uncle, I'll do anything, anything as long as I can get something to eat," she mumbled at each stop.

It was toward the end of the tenth lunar month. The fishing folk looked at Lin Shi, but asked no questions. Most of them said to her out of kindness: "Wait till next month, when the squid come. If there's a lot, you can help pick and sort them. For now, there aren't enough fish even for us. How can we afford to hire someone? Besides, even if we could, there isn't any work to do."

Lin Shi walked past one mud hut after another. The waning light from the setting sun was weak and short-lived. The dark mud huts soon merged into the twilight, becoming isolated shadows. The fishing folk valued their electricity too much to turn on their weak, five-watt light bulbs at this hour, so the entire area was soon covered by a blanket of darkness. But not far off there was light coming from a brick-walled compound that stood in stark contrast to the mud huts around it.

Lin Shi walked over to the compound, went inside, and headed toward the main house. A man seated at an Eight-Immortal table was doing calculations on an abacus.

"Kind Uncle," Lin Shi repeated her mumbled plea, "I'll do anything, anything as long as I can get something to eat."

The man turned to look at her. He was young, with a square

face. He looked Lin Shi over carefully, then turned back and shouted into the house, calling out a name.

"Where are you from?" he asked. "Where do you live? What can you do?"

Lin Shi was about to reply when a woman appeared, carrying a tray with some bowls of rice and food. As soon as she saw Lin Shi, she turned to the man and spoke to him in a low voice.

Lin Shi heard snatches of the conversation: "Pig-Butcher Chen's . . ." "Wanted to beat up Ah-qing that time." "Auntie Ah-wang . . . not get involved." The man listened, nodding his head from time to time. He took the food from the woman, filled a bowl to the top with rice, and walked up to Lin Shi.

"We don't need any help right now," he said in a gentle, deliberate tone, "but you go ahead and eat this rice. You can go on back home after you've finished."

Lin Shi didn't want to take the bowl from him. "I can do laundry," she blurted out, "and I can do cleaning . . ."

But when she saw the determined look on the man's face, she took the bowl from him, turned, and rushed out of the compound. Once outside, she squatted down and began shoveling the rice into her mouth with her hand. When it was gone, she realized that the empty bowl presented a problem—she couldn't very well go back into the compound. Finally, she furtively put it just inside the gate, then got to her feet. But she didn't know where she should go.

The night air was bone-chilling cold. Bleak, icy winds shrieked as they gusted. The bright half-moon—it was nearly the fifteenth of the month—hung high in the sky, its light, bluish white and ghostly pale, shining everywhere. Lin Shi walked ahead aimlessly. There wasn't a sound to be heard or a person to be seen. It was as though the whole of Lucheng had disappeared, leaving her alone in the bitter cold between the deserted sky and the desolate earth.

She kept walking until she caught a glimpse of a few mud huts in which the lights were still lit. She considered going to her uncle's house, but as soon as the idea occurred to her, she recalled that on the day of her wedding, Uncle had made it clear that he wanted no further involvement with her, that she was not to come back—ever. She kept walking, as though in a trance, but in time the severe cold and the drowsiness that come from a full belly began to get to her. Without realizing it, she started tracing her steps homeward.

The next day, Chen Jiangshui returned home a little before noon, bringing with him a big piece of lean pork and a large fish. Lin Shi was so wild with joy that she missed the dark look on his face. She reached out to take the food from him, but he was in no hurry to hand it over.

"Ah-wang says you've been going around looking for work," he said darkly. "Now the entire population of Chencuo is laughing at me for not being able to feed my own wife." Lin Shi tensed with alarm, expecting Chen Jiangshui to reach out and hit her. Instinctively, she backed up.

"Don't worry, I'm not going to hit you." Chen Jiangshui's eyes, buried deep in folds of flesh, gleamed maliciously. "Okay, since you want some work, tomorrow I'll take you to the slaughterhouse. It so happens that they need someone to clean the entrails."

Lin Shi let out an involuntary scream, but Chen Jiangshui paid no attention as he went into the other room, and she sagged down into a crouch, her strength drained. The horror stories she had heard about the slaughterhouse crowded into her mind. In the bitter cold, she wrapped her arms tightly around her bent knees, curled up into a ball, and remained motionless until nearly noon. Then, when the sun was directly overhead, she hurriedly got to her feet to prepare lunch. The harsh wintry air in the room began to warm up as she rekindled the fire, and the stove radiated heat that she could feel without actually touching it with her hand. The familiar routine of kitchen work put her at ease, and in the reflected glow of the fire, her face flushed, she prepared a big lunch.

Chen Jiangshui acted calm all day long. During dinner he drank some wine and hummed his favorite tunes. He sat on the chair with one leg folded under him, tapping the floor with his left foot, often keeping rhythm to his humming, which, at its best, amounted to no more than a few phrases:

> *My darling girl—by the hand—into her chamber*
> *What others—may say—pay no heed*

Lin Shi leaned up against the stove, which offered little warmth now that the fire was out. By placing her hands on the stovetop, she could still feel a hint of warmth, which penetrated her palms slowly and evenly. But after a short while, the residual warmth dissipated and the stove was so cold that she seemed to be heating it with the warmth from her palms instead of the other way around.

The next day, before it was even light outside, Lin Shi was roused from her sleep by Chen Jiangshui's shouts. It had been so long since she had gotten up this early that she was only half awake as she obeyed Chen Jiangshui's orders to get dressed. It wasn't until she was on her way out the door that she realized they were going to the slaughterhouse. She tried to resist, but soon gave in after some angry words from Chen Jiangshui and a couple of slaps.

Lin Shi walked behind Chen Jiangshui, stumbling along in the dark. As they passed through the numerous alleys and small lanes, it suddenly occurred to her how unfamiliar her surroundings were, not at all like the Lucheng she had lived in for so many years. At that moment, all she could do was follow closely behind

Chen Jiangshui. He was, after all, the only kin she had—he was still her husband. Blasts of predawn wind, the coldest of all, struck her full in the face.

The lights of the slaughterhouse appeared in the distance. Bright and glittery, they glowed in the midst of a vast darkness of fields, putting Lin Shi's heart at ease. But the minute she entered the slaughterhouse, she was assailed by a sharp, acrid stench, the endless cries of squealing pigs, and the sight of people crisscrossing back and forth. For a moment she could hardly make out anything in the dim light that bathed everything in a yellow haze. Vapor from water boiling in an enormous vat formed a spreading fog. Flickering human shapes were reflected in the film of water on the floor. These sights, these sounds—they all seemed far, far away, like images in a dream, totally without substance.

Chen Jiangshui disappeared as soon as he led Lin Shi inside. She stood dazed. For a brief moment she truly believed that she had entered a dreamworld and that what she was witnessing now could be nothing less than the hell so often described to her by Auntie Ah-wang.

Just then Chen Jiangshui reappeared, seemingly out of nowhere. In the dim yellow light she saw the sharp gleaming knife in his hand as it plunged into the gullet of a pig, followed by a prolonged raspy squeal and a great deal of blood gushing out of a wound. The scenario was repeated over and over again. Finally, when all the screams had died away and the blood had stopped flowing, Lin Shi watched Chen Jiangshui trace a downward motion with his knife—miraculously, immaculately, without even a trickle of bloody liquid, the abdomen of one of the pigs parted, and from inside, a mass of pulsating gray innards of varying thicknesses spilled out along with some dark-colored organs. It was such a departure from what she had imagined, so devoid of the blood she had expected to see, that she was more convinced than ever that she was caught up in a dream.

But then Chen Jiangshui came walking up to her with an armful of organs and intestines, which he thrust toward her without saying a word. Automatically, she reached out and took them from him. They were soft and sticky to the touch, and still quite warm.

The spongy texture, the heavy bulk, the feeling of warmth, the suffocating stench that assailed her nose—Lin Shi suddenly comprehended the fact that this was not a dream. As the realization began to sink in, her mind became crowded with gushing blood and long, piercing screams, making the whole scene all too real. Looking down, she saw that she was holding a wriggling mass of intestines in her arms, one long coil of which had spilled out of her embrace and was dangling in midair.

With an agonizing scream, she keeled over backwards before she even had time to toss away the things in her arms; her eyes rolled back in her head and a white froth began drooling from her mouth.

Lin Shi was taken home on a two-wheeled cart used to transport pigs. However, shortly before noon, someone in Chencuo saw her kneeling beside the well, her hair all dishevelled and her eyes red, bowing to passersby and pleading with them:

"Kindhearted people, have pity, be merciful! Give me a coin so I can offer a decent sacrifice to my mother. My mother was raped, so she killed herself by jumping down a well. The tongues in my stomach tell me she's drenched from head to toe. She has no clothes, nothing to eat. She's famished. I have to burn some clothes for her, fix her a big meal, let her have something to wear, not let her go hungry. Kindhearted people, have pity, be merciful! Give me a coin . . ."

She repeated this over and over to anyone she saw, as though she were singing a refrain. At noon in Chencuo the fishing folk were still out at sea, leaving only the older women at home. Many of them came out to try to talk to Lin Shi. Oblivious to what they were saying, she kept bowing and pleading with everyone who passed by. After gathering round and watching her for a while, one of the women went to look for Chen Jiangshui, but he wasn't at home and no one knew where to find him. After a while, the crowd broke up and went home.

Several people from outside the area, people who didn't know Lin Shi, thought she was a beggar. Seeing how pitiful she looked and what a dutiful daughter she appeared to be, they gave her a few coppers. The afternoon sun had begun its descent in the west when Lin Shi, clutching the few coppers in her hand, got up to go, leaving behind the few curious children who had been watching her the whole time.

Chen Jiangshui heard about Lin Shi's strange behavior from Auntie Ah-wang, but by the time he rushed home, night had already fallen. He and some of the assistants from the slaughter-house had downed a few extra cups of wine at dinner to wash away that morning's residue of bad luck. As he stepped through the front door, his eyes were greeted by a smoke-filled room dimly lit by the weak light bulb, his nose by the strong smell of burning incense. Through the haze he was barely able to make out a few colored papier-mâché effigies standing stiffly on the Eight-Immortals table. The figures, which were all a foot or so tall, had highly rouged flat faces and were dressed in brightly colored paper clothing. Additional suits of paper clothing—purple shirts over loose-fitting green pants—were lying alongside, and next to the paper clothing were bowls of rice and other food, all covered by a layer of incense ash.

The sight of these brightly colored paper figures gave Chen Jiangshui such a fright that he broke out in a sweat. But when he spotted Lin Shi praying on her knees before the altar, he strode over, grabbed her by the hair, and began beating her on her face and head, cursing angrily: "Screw your mother! So, I've caught you burning effigies to my spirit before I'm even dead. Trying to put a curse on me, are you? Fuck!"

Lin Shi didn't reply. She didn't cry. She just turned back and continued praying on her knees.

"I've had enough of your phony concern, all that crap about praying for your mother. Up your old lady's cunt. Fuck her! I'm the one you're out to get!"

"Don't you say bad things about my mother."

In the midst of bowing, Lin Shi raised her head. Her hair tumbled down over her ghostly pale face. Although she was staring vacantly ahead, her eyes were aglow with an eerie light. Straining to focus her attention, she said slowly: "Don't you dare fuck my mother . . ."

"What did you say! I'll fuck your mother's cunt, and when I'm done with her, it'll be your turn!"

The slightly tipsy Chen Jiangshui was feeling very pleased with himself as he said over and over: "I'll fuck your mother, then I'll fuck you!" He dragged her into the bedroom, tearing her clothes off along the way. Then he took his butcher knife, which he carried with him at all times, and brandished it under her nose.

"If you don't scream and yell this time, I'll fix you good with this knife."

"No, don't fuck my mother . . ." Lin Shi mumbled, shrinking back.

"You gonna scream or not?" He mounted her. "If you don't, I'll take you back to the slaughterhouse and really show you something good."

Lin Shi didn't struggle; she just whimpered softly like a small animal. It sounded to Chen Jiangshui like moaning, and he was satisfied. When he finished, he rolled off her and, as always, was asleep in no time. The gleaming butcher knife lay on the bed next to his hand.

Lin Shi sat up and wrapped her arms around her bent knees. She stared vacantly at the pale moonbeam streaming in through the tiny window. The ghostly light inched slowly across the bed. As though drawn by it, she stared at the light without blinking. When the moonbeam passed over the blade of the knife, there was a flash of light. Lin Shi reached out and picked up the knife.

The broad-backed, thin-edged knife was extraordinarily heavy. Lin Shi gripped it with both hands and stabbed downwards. In the surrounding darkness, the face of a man in a soldier's uniform flashed into view—there was a scar running from his eyebrow to his chin. Then it was a squealing, struggling pig with a butcher knife buried at an angle in its gullet, buckets of dark red blood gushing from the wound, the animal's body wracked with convulsions.

How could there be so much blood? Wasn't it ever going to stop? She couldn't figure it out. Recalling what she had seen at the slaughterhouse, she rolled the head over to one side, but the blood didn't flow to that side alone, as she had expected. The warm, salty, sticky blood just kept gushing, spraying her face as it splattered in all directions.

The geysers of blood began to converge, and for a brief moment, what looked like a single bloodred pillar penetrated the inky darkness. I must be dreaming. Lin Shi rubbed her eyes. Suddenly the convulsions started, crumbling the pillar, and sending its thick blood splattering in all directions.

I must be dreaming, Lin Shi thought. There isn't this much blood when they butcher the pigs at the slaughterhouse. I'll open up the abdomen and see. More blood—more sticky blood. And the innards, nothing like the ones she had seen, all clean and whole and not stained by a drop of blood—no, these were immersed in blood, gory blood.

She reached in and scooped out a handful of intestines, all warm and long and tangled together. She scooped out more and more, finally coming up with a tangled mass of noodles. Countless bright red tongues noisily jabbered on and on. She raised the knife and hacked and hacked until the tongues went away.

I must be dreaming, she thought. I should cut off the head next. As she hacked away with the knife, she kept thinking, I must be dreaming. Why else would there be so much blood? She hacked away with the knife. Hacking, hacking, she reached the feet. Parts close to the body still had big chunks of meat on them. The pig's feet must not be done yet, that's why the center is still red, with all that strong-smelling bloody liquid draining from it. She chopped a few more times until it was all reduced to a pulpy mound of flesh and blood. No need to worry about that, she thought, as she raised the knife and started in on another part.

Finally, seeing that it had all been cut into pieces, Lin Shi sat down. The ghostly white moonlight had retreated to the doorway. It'll all be over soon, and then everything will be fine, she thought. It was only then that she felt the hunger that had been gnawing at her insides. Her mouth was filled with a sour liquid.

Lin Shi let the butcher knife drop from her hand and crawled out of the room over to the stove. With a practiced hand, she started a fire, took the paper figures and clothing that were on the makeshift altar, and burned them all, one by one. In the fiery glow she took the bowls of sacrificial food and, crouching beside the stove, ate ravenously until she was so stuffed she couldn't swallow another bite. She leaned up against the warm foot of the stove and fell into a deep, dreamless sleep.

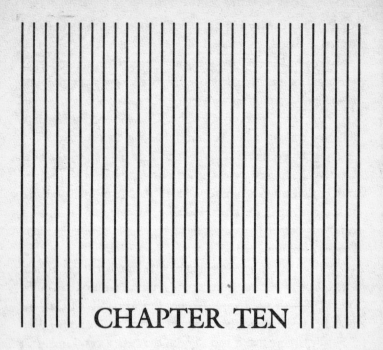

CHAPTER TEN

For the better part of a year, Auntie Ah-wang's house became Lucheng's gossip center. First there were the people from Chencuo, then the investigators, followed by people from every district of the city, all of whom congregated at Auntie Ah-wang's. Most of them asked: "Did you see the murder?"

"If I had, do you think I'd have let her go through with it? Pig-Butcher Chen saved my life once, and I owed him. He was my benefactor, you know."

Auntie Ah-wang still talked in a raspy voice, and she was as attentive as ever to details. Her hair was swept back into a shiny, smooth bun, her white blouse was stiffly starched.

The next thing the people asked was: "Is it true that you saw her trying to dispose of the body?"

"It sure is, and that's the reason justice was done." Auntie Ah-wang followed this with a detailed narration: "That Lin Shi, ever since she came over as a bride, I knew there was something queer about her, so I kept my eye on her. When I noticed that nobody was entering or leaving their house, which is right next door, I went over to investigate. My god! The entire place, even the ceiling and walls, was covered with blood, dried blood. I saw that wretched Lin Shi stuffing something or other into a big rattan chest. Then in the middle of the night, she slipped out to the patches of reeds down by the beach to dispose of whatever it was. I watched her dispose of one piece after another—hands, a head, everything—then come back for a second load. I couldn't let her get away with that, so I reported her right away."

Most of the people stood around waiting to hear more, so Auntie Ah-wang related everything there was to know about Lin Shi, beginning with her mother. And for the women in the crowd, she lowered her voice and said: "She even stopped moaning toward the end. I wonder if that means that Pig-Butcher Chen couldn't control her any longer. Heh-heh, I even heard him accuse her once of taking a lover!"

"Did she really take a lover?" one of her curious listeners asked.

"You know the old saying 'There's no murder without adultery,'" Auntie Ah-wang intoned solemnly. "Just look how it turned out—mother and daughter both in trouble for the same reason. I tell you, we women really have to watch our step."

Her listeners nodded their heads in agreement.

"Not that I want to sing my own praises, but not long ago there was that problem with the hanging ghost. Luck was with me and I escaped with my life, but Pig-Butcher Chen, he wasn't so lucky."

Then she added: "'If the cosmos is not in order, what hope is there for ethics?' In my opinion, Lin Shi didn't have enough sense to count her blessings. Just think, by marrying Pig-Butcher Chen she had no parents-in-law to lord it over her, no brothers- or sisters-in-law to care for, and no need to go to sea or work in the fields. She could eat whatever she wanted without lifting a finger. I don't know how many generations of virtuous cultivation it takes to be able to live that kind of life, but she didn't know a good thing when she had it, and that's why she wound up like she did."

Auntie Ah-wang paused momentarily, then added contemptuously: "All a woman has to do is put up with it a while, and it'll pass. Who ever heard of someone yelling and carrying on until everybody in the neighborhood knows and no other woman is willing to speak up for her? Honestly!"

Sooner or later, even gossip has to come to an end. When the people around her were about to leave, Auntie Ah-wang sighed and concluded her tale: "It was her cruel fate, that's what it was. The mother got into trouble, and since theirs was a family short on luck, the daughter wound up committing murder for the same reason. It was in the cards, I tell you, it was divine retribution!"

"How true! It was divine retribution!" the others agreed.

FOR THE BEST IN PAPERBACKS, LOOK FOR THE 🐧

In every corner of the world, on every subject under the sun, Penguin represents quality and variety – the very best in publishing today.

For complete information about books available from Penguin – including Puffins, Penguin Classics and Arkana – and how to order them, write to us at the appropriate address below. Please note that for copyright reasons the selection of books varies from country to country.

In the United Kingdom: Please write to *Dept E.P., Penguin Books Ltd, Harmondsworth, Middlesex, UB7 0DA.*

If you have any difficulty in obtaining a title, please send your order with the correct money, plus ten per cent for postage and packaging, to *PO Box No 11, West Drayton, Middlesex*

In the United States: Please write to *Dept BA, Penguin, 299 Murray Hill Parkway, East Rutherford, New Jersey 07073*

In Canada: Please write to *Penguin Books Canada Ltd, 2801 John Street, Markham, Ontario L3R 1B4*

In Australia: Please write to the *Marketing Department, Penguin Books Australia Ltd, P.O. Box 257, Ringwood, Victoria 3134*

In New Zealand: Please write to the *Marketing Department, Penguin Books (NZ) Ltd, Private Bag, Takapuna, Auckland 9*

In India: Please write to *Penguin Overseas Ltd, 706 Eros Apartments, 56 Nehru Place, New Delhi, 110019*

In the Netherlands: Please write to *Penguin Books Netherlands B.V., Postbus 195, NL–1380AD Weesp*

In West Germany: Please write to *Penguin Books Ltd, Friedrichstrasse 10–12, D–6000 Frankfurt/Main 1*

In Spain: Please write to *Alhambra Longman S.A., Fernandez de la Hoz 9, E–28010 Madrid*

In Italy: Please write to *Penguin Italia s.r.l., Via Como 4, I-20096 Pioltello (Milano)*

In France: Please write to *Penguin Books Ltd, 39 Rue de Montmorency, F-75003 Paris*

In Japan: Please write to *Longman Penguin Japan Co Ltd, Yamaguchi Building, 2–12–9 Kanda Jimbocho, Chiyoda-Ku, Tokyo 101*

FOR THE BEST IN PAPERBACKS, LOOK FOR THE

PENGUIN INTERNATIONAL WRITERS

Gamal Al-Ghitany	**Zayni Barakat**
Wang Anyi	**Baotown**
Joseph Brodsky	**Marbles: A Play in Three Acts**
Shusaku Endo	**The Samurai**
	Scandal
	Wonderful Fool
Ida Fink	**A Scrap of Time**
Miklós Haraszti	**The Velvet Prison**
Ivan Klíma	**My First Loves**
	A Summer Affair
Jean Levi	**The Chinese Emperor**
Harry Mulisch	**Last Call**
Cees Nooteboom	**A Song of Truth and Semblance**
Luise Rinser	**Prison Journal**
Anton Shammas	**Arabesques**
Josef Škvorecký	**The Cowards**
Tatyana Tolstoya	**On the Golden Porch and Other Stories**
Elie Wiesel	**Twilight**
Zhang Xianliang	**Half of Man is Woman**

FOR THE BEST IN PAPERBACKS, LOOK FOR THE 🐧

A SELECTION OF FICTION AND NON-FICTION

The Dictionary of the Khazars   Milorad Pavić

'Borges and Nabokov, Singer and Calvino, Eco's *The Name of the Rose* – Pavić's novel conjures up images (dreams?) of some of our century's most enthralling imaginative literature ... I would say that in its teasing way it is a masterpiece' – *Sunday Times*

Travels in the Drifting Dawn   Kenneth White

Beginning in the underground London of the sixties and the Glasgow of the same period, where he was a 'non-secret agent' for William Burroughs' and Alex Trocchi's Project Sigma, the wanderings of Kenneth White have carried him from Ireland to North Africa to the very edges of western culture.

My Father's Moon   Elizabeth Jolley

Vera Wright was a boarding-school girl, then a nurse in wartime England, the era of air-raids, rationing and tangos on the gramophone, when all the girls waited for letters, and some of them waited for love.

Einstein's Monsters   Martin Amis

'This collection of five stories and an introductory essay ... announces an obsession with nuclear weapons; it also announces a new tonality in Amis's writing' – John Lanchester in the *London Review of Books*

In the Heart of the Country   J. M. Coetzee

In a web of reciprocal oppression in colonial South Africa, a white sheep farmer makes a bid for salvation in the arms of a black concubine, while his embittered daughter dreams of and executes a bloody revenge. Or does she?

Baumgartner's Bombay   Anita Desai

'Hugo Baumgartner, the central character in Anita Desai's dazzling new novel, is a wandering Jew all his life ... Too dark for Hitler's society, he is too fair for India; he remains a *firanghi*, a foreigner wherever he goes' – *Daily Telegraph*. 'The achievement of a superior writer' – *Literary Review*

A SELECTION OF FICTION AND NON-FICTION

Cal   Bernard Mac Laverty

Springing out of the fear and violence of Ulster, *Cal* is a haunting love story from a land where tenderness and innocence can only flicker briefly in the dark. 'Mac Laverty describes the sad, straitened, passionate lives of his characters with tremendously moving skill' – *Spectator*

The Rebel Angels   Robertson Davies

A glittering extravaganza of wit, scatology, saturnalia, mysticism and erudite vaudeville. 'The kind of writer who makes you want to nag your friends until they read him so that they can share the pleasure' – *Observer*

Stars of the New Curfew   Ben Okri

'Anarchical energy with authoritative poise … an electrifying collection' – Graham Swift. 'Okri's work is obsessive and compelling, spangled with a sense of exotic magic and haunted by shadows … reality re-dreamt with great conviction' – *Time Out*

The Magic Lantern   Ingmar Bergman

'A kaleidoscope of memories intercut as in a film, sharply written and trimmed to the bone' – *Sunday Times*. 'The autobiography is exactly like the films: beautiful and repulsive; truthful and phoney; constantly startling' – *Sunday Telegraph*. 'Unique, reticent, revealing' – Lindsay Anderson

The Horn   John Clellon Holmes

Edgar Pool is slave to nothing, not even the genius inside him. He lives no life but jazz, no days but nights wrestling swing out of sordidness in the crowded clubs of New York. And out of obsession with the sound of his tenor sax the legend of bop is born… 'The people … are real, the music is thrilling, and the writing is powerful' – *Chicago Tribune*

The News from Ireland   William Trevor

'An ability to enchant as much as chill has made Trevor unquestionably one of our greatest short-story writers' – *The Times*. 'A masterly collection' – *Daily Telegraph*

FOR THE BEST IN PAPERBACKS, LOOK FOR THE 🐧

A SELECTION OF FICTION AND NON-FICTION

The Great Indian Novel   Shashi Tharoor

In a dazzling marriage of Hindu myth and modern history, Sashi Tharoor reinvents India. 'Vastly enjoyable ... a *tour de force* of considerable brilliance ... *The Great Indian Novel* never fails to hold our attention' – *The Times Literary Supplement*

The Purple Decades   Tom Wolfe

From Surfers to Moonies, from *The Electric Kool-Aid Acid Test* to *The Right Stuff*, a technicolour retrospective from the foremost chronicler of the gaudiest period in American history.

Still Life   A. S. Byatt

Frederica Potter, 'doomed to be intelligent', plunges into the university life of 1950s Cambridge greedy for knowledge, sex and love. In Yorkshire her sister Stephanie has abandoned academe for the cosy frustration of the family. 'Affords enormous and continuous pleasure' – Anita Brookner

The Moronic Inferno   Martin Amis

'Really good reading and sharp, crackling writing. Amis has a beguiling mixture of confidence and courtesy, and most of his literary judgments – often twinned with interviews – seem sturdy, even when caustic, without being bitchy for the hell of it' – *Guardian*

The Silence in the Garden   William Trevor

'Subtle, intricate and beautiful ... Mr Trevor's compassion for his characters ... makes this novel of decline and melancholy decay an affirmation of the goodness and rich variety of life ... No-one interested in what fiction can do to illuminate and enrich life should fail to read this book' – Allan Massie

The Guide   R. K. Narayan

Raju, recently released from prison, used to be India's most corrupt tourist guide. Then a peasant mistakes him for a holy man – and gradually he begins to play the part. He succeeds so well that God himself intervenes to put his new holiness to the test.